Mrs A. Fullington

The Way of The Transgressor

John Jack

PUBLISHED BY
THE WEST PUBLISHING CO.
APOLLO, PA.

Copyright 1948
The West Publishing Co.

Introduction

Why another book? Are there not plenty on the market now? Those questions could well be asked in fairness. But here is the reason for "The Way of The Transgressor".

We needed a story to run in the American Holiness Journal. After several futile attempts to get some one to write one, we tried it ourselves. It was with no thought of any superior ability, or even average ability, with which we tackled the job. But we did our best to keep the story alive, interesting, and still spiritual.

From the very first people said, "You should print that story in book form." The longer the story ran the greater became the number of requests. So here it is.

John Jack

*To
Prudie*

Contents

Chapter I
No Love Is Lost 11

Chapter II
Gathering the Evidence 24

Chapter III
The Revival Is On 32

Chapter IV
The Parting of the Ways 39

Chapter V
The Trap Springs 49

Chapter VI
Easier This Way 66

Chapter VII
Only In Thoughts 80

Chapter VIII
The End of the Trail 92

Chapter IX
Johnson Gets the Breaks 106

Chapter X
Big Tom Strikes Again 116

Chapter XI
The Way It Goes 129

NANCY

The light of the righteous rejoiceth: but the lamp of the wicked shall be put out. Prov. 13:9.

CHAPTER I

NO LOVE IS LOST

The steam engine coughed its way through the very last cut for the day. Earl lifted the dog, rolled the tie off onto the rolls, pushed it to the lumber truck and tipped it on.

Bill Johnson, the bulky sawyer yelled, "Shut her down!" Sandy pushed the throttle and the whirling wheels coasted to a stop.

Things were just beginning to hum nicely around Johnson's mill—just getting set up and ready to do some real cutting. That Kelly tract was a good one—as timber went in that section of the country—and a fairly large one for a portable outfit.

The mill, located at the mouth of a little hollow at one side of the tract, was the center of the miniature settlement that was built by the workmen. Just back of the skidway, along the bank, stood the shanty that was occupied by Bill Johnson, the sawyer and the owner of the little plant, and his daughter, Nancy, a girl just past seventeen. It was a good deal better than the average run of dwellings that were built around a mill job. You came into a large room that served as kitchen, dining room, and master bedroom. Off to the right a door opened into Nancy's room.

THE WAY OF THE TRANSGRESSOR

It was nothing elaborate, but it was tidy, clean, and homelike. Nancy was putting the finishing touches to the evening meal. Tonight it was saurkraut and dumplings, with a man-size piece of apple pie by each plate.

Nancy stepped to the door, pulled the latch and swung it open. The cool autumn breeze fanned her face, and played through the wavy brown hair. She cupped her hands to her mouth and shouted, "Supper, Dad! The dumplings will be getting cold."

Bill Johnson was helping with the final straightening out before the crew left the mill and each man headed for his lodging place. As Bill walked up the little path to the lodge, he was joined by the teamster, Ham. That's all anybody seemed to know about him—"Ham Jacobs", he said, when asked how to make out his pay check, and that it had been for the past five years he had been driving Johnson's team.

"Tomorrow's 'bout the last I can keep 'er goin', Bill. Have ter get that old cat pawing right quick now."

Bill hung his head a bit and studied as he walked to the door where Nancy was waiting for him. This log skidding was a Jonah. There under a big white oak stood the 'cat'—and she was a good one too—but there wasn't a man on the job would drive her, except himself and he was more than busy at the mill. He had been looking for a man "all over creation" as he said, but none would do it. The last driver got tangled up in the winch and lost a leg over it. Not a man on the job would touch it now.

If he was worried, he didn't show it, as he came to

the door and placed a big rough hand gently on Nancy's shoulder.

"All ready, Nanc?" he asked in a good natured way.

"Ready and waiting!"

Little was said as the two men washed, and took their places at the table and began to eat. Then Ham broke the silence in his usual blunt way, "Draggin' hard over this dry ground. Little rain help a heap."

Bill didn't get to answer for just then someone knocked on the door.

Nancy was to her feet, "Wonder who wants you now, dad", she remarked on her way to the door.

"Hello, Mam! Could I see Bill Johnson?"

Nancy was unable to answer or to move. For a second, she just stood and stared at the young man. He must be full six feet, and all there too, you could see at a glance.

"Er——oh, yes, come in," she stammered. "He's just eating supper."

"Want to see me, did you say? I'm Bill Johnson. Have a chair." With this Bill swung around on his homemade chair and faced the newcomer.

"Yes, I'm looking for a job. Blake's the name. Charles Blake."

He stretched out a big hand and took hold of one equally as big and Bill Johnson knew he was looking at and shaking hands with a man. He knew men when he saw them.

"Well, what can you do, young fellow?" queried Johnson.

THE WAY OF THE TRANSGRESSOR

"Last job, up on Spruce Ridge, I drove a cat. But I reckon I can do most anything 'round a lumber job."

It was hard for Bill not to seem over anxious about this new prospect.

"Well, I reckon we could handle another man around here somewhere. Might let you try the cat. Had any supper?"

The reply was no. The invitation was extended and accepted. Ham and Bill both tried in vain to get something of Blake's background. Beyond the job on Spruce Ridge it was sealed.

"How big a job have you got here?" Blake asked.

"Couple million or around that," Bill replied. "Nice stuff, mostly oak and pine, but rough in spots."

There were no formal introductions, but Blake soon gathered that Nancy was Bill's daughter, and Ham was one of the hands. Supper finished, Bill pushed back his chair and remarked, "There's a couple of tops and a few logs laying out there in the lumber yard that I think I'll jerk out so we can get some bigger docks built tomorrow."

Ham shoved back his chair, "I'd like ter help you all right, Bill, but Ted pulled a shoe, and I'll have to drive it ter be ready ter hit 'er in the morning."

"That's all right, Ham, you go right ahead."

"If I can be of any help, I'll be right with you," Blake spoke in an easy deep voice.

"Sure, may as well come along". Bill, in reality, was only thinking up something to do where he could find out whether or not Blake could handle the 'cat'. If he could,

THE WAY OF THE TRANSGRESSOR

the cutters should go on up the hollow a ways instead of working right around the mill.

"She's a nice one all right!" spoke up Blake, "Not been working her much lately."

"No, been doing most of it with the horses—short skids."

Bill opened the priming cups, poured in a little gasoline. By that time Blake had adjusted the magneto and had ahold of the crank. When ready he gave her a couple of quarter turns and she was off.

Blake stood back, he was anxious to get his hands on those levers. But Bill crawled into the seat, opened the governor a little, and started. Blake followed.

Bill backed it up to a big white oak top and Blake threw the chain around and stepped back. Bill stepped down and looked around as if wondering where to put the top.— Then pointing to an open place, said to Blake, "Crawl on and haul her through that hole over there."

Blake swung limply into the seat, hauled her back into low, opened the governors and started her off as gently as an old time engineer starts off the "Clipper". The chain tightened, limbs cracked and snapped, the governors opened, but the big 'cat' had more than she could break loose. Blake threw it into reverse, swung it around until it was pulling the top in a twist. It gave a little ground, then locked. Now he hauled it back the other way. Then looking at the chain, he saw it was a good heavy one, he swung her straight ahead, gave her a little slack and opened her up. The chain tightened with a jerk; limbs cracked; the governors opened; the top broke her hold and let go.

THE WAY OF THE TRANSGRESSOR

Bill smiled, "He'll do," he thought to himself.

When, in about an hour, the two men stood by the tractor as she coughed out the last fuel in the carburator, Bill was satisfied that if Blake stayed on the job, there would be logs. But he may be just another rambler—never stay long any place.

"There's two bunks in Ham's shanty, Blake. Reckon you can sleep with him tonight. Stop by our cabin and get a couple of blankets." Bill walked up around the mill and took a look for any fire, while Blake leisurely made his way to Johnson's cabin.

The door was open and Nancy saw him coming.

"Mr. Johnson said I should stop here to see about a couple of blankets for tonight. Didn't bring much with me."

"Of course you may have some blankets," Nancy replied, and was soon pulling out the necessary bedding from a trunk in the back of the room. She wrapped it in a bundle and handed it to Blake.

"Hope you like our little settlement, Mr. Blake", Nancy said smiling.

"Thank you mam, reckon I will," Blake said easily. He had seen a smile like that before, but it had been a long time ago—so long ago that it seemed it belonged to another world. He turned easily and walked in a slow gate toward the cabin that Johnson had pointed out as Ham's. He knocked and Ham answered, "Come on in."

"Room for another fellow in here tonight, Ham?"

"Sure thing, Blake. I don't like ter stay by myself no how".

THE WAY OF THE TRANSGRESSOR

Blake unfolded the bundle Nancy had given him—clean sheets, a pillow and two blankets. After the bunk was in shape, he told Ham he was going to look around a little.

Blake turned up a skidding road that led back toward the standing timber. He wanted to walk. His mind was in a turmoil, and there was a strange sensation flooding his soul. Bill Johnson had reminded him of his dad, Nancy had a lot in common with his kid sister. Memory was all that was left to him now—since that night of the tragedy. With a shudder he recalled that night when he had come home to find their cabin in flames. There had been an investigation by the law, but nothing had ever come of it. He could never understand why his dad hadn't gotten out of the little shack. They had told him that there was a dent in his father's head. That could have been caused by a falling piece of lumber during the fire, but somehow he doubted that. The more he thought about it the more he doubted that explanation. As his suspicions grew, one name stood out in his mind—the name of Eric James. He clenched his fists as he recalled the night his father had been forced to throw James out of the shanty because of his misbehavior when Martha had refused to marry him, and to have anything more to do with him.

Blake came now to the end of the road. He could see where Ham had pulled out the last load of logs. Perhaps when morning came he could lose himself in his work again. That had been his only relief in the past. The search was on! Eric James would sooner or later gravitate to some camp. Sitting down on a big oak stump, he buried his head in his hands. "Oh God!" he moaned. It was not in profanity, but rather more like a prayer—the prayer of desperation. He could plainly remember how his mother prayed. His father had been a man of prayer, and Martha had planned to go to some place or another as a missionary. As for himself, religion had never taken up much of his time—he figured that there was plenty of time later on to think of God. But right now as the shadows engulfed the forest, the shadows of despair seemed to engulf his soul and he was needing some help that he hardly knew where to find.

The soft October breeze was sifting the leaves over the ground and playing a sad cadence among the tall pines that stood immediately in back of him. He lifted his head and watched the sun shoot its last rays over the earth and drop beyond the horizon in a pot of molten gold. A squirrel barked to its mate from a tall oak and then hurried off to its nest. Blake saw the fleecy clouds take on the color of molten gold.

How long after that he sat there he didn't realize until he heard the barking of a fox through the timber. Then he became aware that it was dusk and hurried down the trail to the lumber shanties.

* * *

The morning broke clear and bright. The sun lighted up the hillside of standing timber in the gayest of autumn colors gave its promise of a clear October day. Blake helped Ham harness the team and together they went to Johnson's cabin for breakfast.

Nancy was in a gay mood. She greeted Blake with a smile, "Looks like you'll have a nice day to start with dad."

"Yeh, I'm glad to get back to work again. Can't loaf long. Get too restless. Have too much time to think."

THE WAY OF THE TRANSGRESSOR

He had talked plenty he thought, and stopped. He was not a talker. But it seemed that if he didn't unload his heart soon it would burst.

Johnson greeted him with a cheery, "Good morning, Blake".

Breakfast over, they left the cabin. Ham went for the team; Blake followed Johnson up to the mill. Bill looked a little puzzled as to the next move. He prized that "cat" and was pondering whether or not to allow Blake to try it. He guessed he would.

"The sled is out under that maple, there Blake. The chains and binders are in the tool box. The fuel is in those drums there, oil in the five gallon can."

"O. K., Bill," and Blake was off.

There were logs that day—plenty of them. Before evening came there was a little stock pile started above the skids. Blake and Ham made a good team.

The mill had stopped and Blake was standing on the skidway watching the mill crew finish up their day's work. He had decided to finish his after supper—some tightening up to do. His heart seemed to be at ease—an ease that was to be shortlived.

"What the——are you doing here, Blake!" Blake was stunned. He knew the voice. Its sound sent the chills to playing up and down his spine. He turned to look into the face of a man he hated with a white hot hatred—the face of Eric James.

"Working, I reckon. Do I look like a state boiler inspector?"

19

THE WAY OF THE TRANSGRESSOR

"You don't need to be so sarcastic," retorted James. He slipped up a little closer to Blake and said in a hoarse whisper, "You make sure you keep your lip shut around here or I'll smash in your pretty face!"

Blake turned a ghostly white, clenched his fist and was about to tell James that he could save his wind. He wasn't afraid of his threats, when Johnson called, "Give me a lift here, Blake. I want to shift this head block a little".

That had saved the day—that day. The fire of hatred and animosity still burned—would burn.

Supper at the Johnson cabin that night was anything but a pleasant time for Blake. James had been invited and had joined them. From the conversation Blake gathered that Nancy and James were going to a pie social at the school house—about two miles down the road.

"May as well go along, Mr. Blake," spoke up Nancy. "We're driving Dad's car. There'll be lots of room."

"No, thanks, I have a little work to do on the tractor this evening. The tracks are too loose." Blake was in no mood for much talk. That was about the amount of his part of the supper-time conversation.

The meal finished, Blake excused himself and left. As he went out the door James cut loose with a slur, "We don't like your company any better than you like ours."

Blake didn't reply nor look back. This was not the time—but it would come. He could hear the laughter coming from the cabin now and then as he worked on the tractor. He saw James leave for a cabin up in the hollow and come back a little later. He was wearing the same suit he wore that night his father had thrown him from the cabin up in Little Stony. He unconsciously shuddered and then turned his head as James entered Johnson's cabin. He was heavier than Blake, with powerful arms and massive shoulders. He tapered gradually to the hips. His back was broad at the narrowest point. Blake had seen him crush more than one man. He was a fighting brute when mad. But Blake had no fear. He was confident in his ability to look after himself.

As he threw the tools in the tool box and snapped the lock on it Johnson came up from under husk. "Doing a little tightening myself, Blake. Conveyor was needing a little work in spots. Say Blake, do you know James? You spoke to him this evening as though you did."

Blake thought for a moment. "Yes I know him. He worked for my dad. That was back before the fire." As he spoke James and Nancy came out of the cabin and got into the car that stood waiting.

Nancy waved good-bye to her father.

"We'll wait, if you would still like to go along, Mr. Blake," Nancy spoke in an earnest tone.

"No, thanks, Nancy, I think I'll go to bed early."

"Yeh, he'll have to get ten hours sleep or he'll get low blood pressure." James shot at him as the car pulled out.

Johnson had sensed the feeling between Blake and James. He felt like Blake was a real man; he wasn't too sure about James—not now.

Blake looked at Johnson. Their eyes met, "You look

THE WAY OF THE TRANSGRESSOR

a little like my Dad looked, Bill. He was a real man too. The finest that ever lived."

"Still living?"

"No, he and my sister burned to death in the fire on Little Stoney. Mother is gone too." Blake spoke without looking up. Then he looked at Johnson again, "Bill, I reckon it really isn't any of my business but don't let James go too far with your girl. He just ain't her kind as I can see it."

Johnson didn't answer for a moment. Then he said, "Thank you, Blake, I'll keep my eyes open. See you in the morning."

Johnson went toward the cabin; Blake turned up the hollow. Sleep was out of the question now. He wanted to walk. The feeling of loneliness and despair had left him. Tonight he felt like an angry lion—and the object of his hatred wasn't in reach—not now.

When Blake, hours later, stepped on the little bridge that crossed from the mill side of the hollow over to where Ham's cabin stood, the headlights of the returning car occupied by James and Nancy light up the hollow. Blake dropped off the bridge to keep from being seen. He had no intentions of eavesdropping but he didn't want to be seen, so he lay close to the bank. He heard the car go by; heard the doors close; heard Nancy and James go toward the cabin. Then his blood fairly boiled in his veins, his heart pounded like a triphammer—he could hear James.

"Come on Nanc, you have held me off all evening—all along. You know I love you. I loved you the first day I saw you. Can't you tell me *you* love *me*".

THE WAY OF THE TRANSGRESSOR

"No Eric. Let me think I have only known you a few months. If you cannot act as a gentleman this will be the last." Nancy was cold, indignant. The little attraction she had had to James was fleeing.

"Remember Nancy, that five grand I loaned your Dad. That note comes due in a few weeks. If you say, 'yes' it'll be forgotten. But if you don't it'll be paid or—." He caught himself. Perhaps he had gone too far now.

Nancy said, "Goodnight", and ran into the cabin. She had been afraid of James all evening, now her fears mounted.

James turned and headed for his cabin. When he crossed the bridge, Blake lay flat to the ground. James was mumbling, "I'll bring her under. That five grand'll talk pretty loud yet." Blake watched him until the darkness swallowed up the receding figure. He waited until the lamp was lighted in James' cabin and then he came out of his hiding and silently slipped into his cabin. Ham was asleep and didn't wake. He was glad for that.

He lay awake for a few minutes thinking. Where did James get $5,000? Blake knew him for years. He had never had a cent. His money didn't last from one pay to the next. Then something clicked. "No—he couldn't have!" He found himself sitting up in bed, talking aloud. Ham rolled over; Blake lay back down. Weariness soon brought relief on the wings of sleep and Blake slept—the sleep of a healthy, tired youth.

CHAPTER II

GATHERING THE EVIDENCE

There were logs the next day and the next. Ham and Blake saw to that. The cutters were still a long ways ahead. Ham had told Johnson, "Fine chap, that Blake. Never worked with no better."

It being Sunday, the tired little settlement stirred a bit later than usual. Breakfast at the Johnson cabin was at 8:30 instead of 7 o'clock.

"How about church, this morning, Charles. I found a nice little country church down here along the road. They are starting a revival down there today, too," Nancy said.

"Sounds all right to me. I used to go to Sunday school and Church—that's before Mother died. She always wanted me to go along with the rest of the family. After she died I could never go back. Held kind of a grudge against God for taking her, I guess." Blake was meditative.

"Going along, Dad?" Nancy asked.

"No not this morning. May go this evening."

"Looks like you and I will be the crowd from here this morning Charles." Nancy seemed pleased. "We'll leave about 9:30, so as to be there for Sunday School."

THE WAY OF THE TRANSGRESSOR

Blake welcomed anything that would keep him from thinking. He didn't want to think.

At 9:30 the Johnson car pulled out for the "White Church." It stood on top of a hill about a mile to the south. As they were leaving the church bell began to ring—half hour before service.

Nancy looked prettier than usual this morning. She had on a light blue dress. That's about all Blake could tell you about the way she was dressed, but there was something about her presence that delighted his heart. It reacted on him something like a cool breeze on a summer day.

How long has your mother been dead, Charles?" Nancy asked.

"It's a little more than six years. She died when I was just fourteen; Martha was twelve. We were a sad family for a while. Dad kept things together though. That was his promise to mother. He sure worshipped her." It seemed to do Blake a lot of good to talk a little. For so long he had harbored things in his heart, turned them over in his mind, that it was a relief to unload a little.

"My mother has been dead for just two years. Only those who have gone through it know anything about what it means. But I have dad left; you don't have anyone now." Nancy was earnestly sympathetic.

There was a moment of silence then Blake said, "Right now there seems little left for me. I have one consuming desire that is to uncover the foul play that I think took place in the death of my dad and sister. I mean to leave no stone uncovered until I bring that out."

THE WAY OF THE TRANSGRESSOR

As they were now about to enter the church, Nancy was left to wonder just what Blake meant. They were greeted with a warm welcome as they entered the church and made to feel right at home. As far as Blake was concerned, the service didn't mean much. The Pastor preached about getting things in order for the blessing of God. Like too many folk, Blake stood right in the midst of the very help he needed but didn't give God a chance to slake the thirst of his restless soul.

On the way home little was said until they were almost there and then it was Nancy who broke the silence, "If there is anything I can do to help you, Blake, let me know. Really, you can trust me."

"I'll take you up on that, Nancy. Right now there is something you can do. Could I see you this afternoon sometime?" Blake meant to lose no time. He had stayed at the Johnson mill longer now than he had originally planned, because there he had found Eric James and the riddle was beginning to unwind.

"Sure, I'll see you this afternoon. I can see you right after dinner."

"That will be fine. Suppose we take a walk up the hollow a way, to get where we won't be overheard." Blake was going to follow up this lead. There were some things that he wanted to find out. Perhaps Nancy could tell him. That he had any personal interest in her, never dawned upon him. She was a pleasant companion; she might be able to get more out of James than anyone else.

THE WAY OF THE TRANSGRESSOR

As they got out of the car, Nancy said, "I'll have dinner in a few minutes. You and Ham be over before long."

* * *

Dinner over and dishes done, Nancy and Blake walked leisurely up the trail toward the standing timber. Autumn had on full dress—a gaiety of color that reflected the beauty of their Creator and shewed forth His handiwork in elaborate fashion.

"God must be great and glorious to create so much beauty," Nancy said in an attempt to get the conversation started.

But Blake wasn't in any mood just then to see the color scheme about him. He didn't hear the bark of the squirrel as it protested the coming of strangers into its domain. He was thinking of one thing, an ugly thing that colored his whole world with its ghastly light and wrung the beauty out of everything—vengeance.

"What I wanted to ask you," he began, "may seem a bit surprising to you, but you said this morning you would be willing to be of any help you could in bringing out the facts in my father's death. I overheard a conversation one night that wasn't meant for me. Perhaps I had better explain." With that Blake told Nancy of the night he lay under the bridge and heard the conversation between her and James. By this time they had entered the standing timber. There was an old pine that had been blown out of root. Pointing to it Blake said, "Sit there for a while. I'll lean against this tree here. I like to sit at the trunk of a tree and lean my back against it."

THE WAY OF THE TRANSGRESSOR

"What I wanted to know was when James came here." He began to seek out the information he desired.

Nancy studied a minute then replied, "Just about a year ago. But you don't think that he had anything to do with your father's death, do you?"

Blake made no reply to her question. "About a year ago?" he thought. "Just about a month after the fire." After a moment's silence Blake said, "Now how about the five thousand dollars; when did he make that loan to your dad?"

"I can't remember exactly. It was just a little while after he came here though. Dad needed it to finish paying off the timber. Dad says there is sometime to go on that and that he'll be able to meet it all right."

"Yes, I don't doubt that your dad will be able to take care of it all right. He has almost enough pine cut already to do that." Things were beginning to take shape in Blake's mind now. He was certain that Eric James had never come into possession of that money in any honorable sort of a way. But how to prove anything was a different matter. He would stay here at the Johnson mill a little longer, longer than he had originally planned. His hunch that James would hunt out another lumber camp after leaving his father's was right. Evidence would pile up. Blake glanced up at Nancy to find her looking at him with kind inquisitive eyes. His eyes met hers but they did not fall.

"Blake, you know, dad says that things will right themselves in time, if you just keep on doing your best and keep faith in God. I like that idea. Why don't you try it in your case?"

"I had thought of that. But you see a year has gone by and nothing has happened. Then you see, I haven't much faith in God. Not that I don't wish that I had, but it just isn't there. I'm afraid that most of that has gone from me. My soul is bitter; if there is a God, why did all this happen. My dad served God, if ever man did; my sister planned to be a missionary. Then why did all this happen!"

"I can't answer all the questions you ask, Blake. But remember that God is good. Everything He does is good, always good."

"Sounds like it would be wonderful to think that way about things. Dad, I can remember, used to say something about all things working together for good or something like that. But I never could take much stock in it. There is this sure thing though—dad lived it all right. This thing is different. I'm pledged to do this thing if it takes my last drop of blood. I mean to have vengeance!"

"Blake, you sound like an old mountaineer following out a fued. You can find a lot nobler things in life than merely seeking to right an old wrong. I'm even sorry that I told you anything." Nancy was close to tears.

"Let's go," Blake said calmly and helped Nancy to her feet.

For a time they walked in silence. Then Blake said, "I reckon you'll think it none of my business, Nancy, but I must tell you anyhow. I'd never feel right if I didn't and then something unfortunate happened. You can do as you please about it. Eric James just isn't your type. I've known him longer than you. He's a rough customer."

"I appreciate your telling me, Blake. I've felt the same way about it. He really doesn't mean a thing to me. I just went with him a few times to be sociable. That is all in the past. Now, how about going to church tonight?"

"Can't do me any harm I reckon. Maybe you think I'll fall into your way of thinking if I get religious." Blake came near to sarcasm.

"Nothing would suit me better. You know, Jesus Christ makes a special business of fixing up things like this. Why don't you try Him. I'll guarantee you he'll do a real job for you." Nancy was doing her best to seem only slightly interested, but it was hard.

"What do you say we walk to church tonight," was Blake's only answer.

"That will be fine," Nancy replied, hoping it would give her a little more opportunity to talk to him about God. "We'll need to leave about seven o'clock. I'll have supper at six."

By this time they were in sight of the cabin. Overhead floated giant white clouds, now and then covering the autumn sun. The leaves reflected the beauty of the autumn sun in a thousand different hues from the hill sides. Everything seemed in tranquil peace. For a moment Blake let his soul drink in the beauty of the evening. There was no denying the fact, too, that he enjoyed the fellowship of a friend again. Many times he had walked thus through the woods with his father and sister. It seemed only a little while since he had taken one of those walks. But as he gazed down the valley, a figure swung across the bridge and hastened to a cabin on the opposite side of the hollow. Blake recognized the man, he could tell in a minute that cat-like gait—it was Eric James. A surge of hatred ran through the veins of Blake. The account wasn't settled, "Not yet." "One day I'll meet that man. It will be a fight to the finish with no quarter offered or accepted," he thought to himself.

CHAPTER III

THE REVIVAL IS ON

"Just as well put this thing out of my mind for the rest of the evening," thought Charles Blake as he walked across from his shanty to Johnson's where he was to get Nancy. He was looking forward to this evening with a good bit of pleasant anticipation. In fact it had been a long time since he really enjoyed anything.

Nancy was ready and waiting. She seemed in a gay mood as she joined Blake. A child-like faith in the goodness of God and His care for every one of His children gave her a great deal of comfort and delight. One of her favorite verses was "No good thing will He withhold from them that walk uprightly." Somehow it seemed as though that must be more than just an empty utterance.

"It's very pleasant this evening. But it may rain before the night is over," Nancy said in an attempt to open the conversation.

"I hope it doesn't. Rain would turn the skidding road into a mess of muck. I hate to wallow around in mud. But a log skidder has to do a lot of it now and then. Winter is always a mess. You're wet most of the time. It's a funny thing, though, I never seem to get a cold from being wet." Blake replied as they walked out of the lumber camp to the road.

THE WAY OF THE TRANSGRESSOR

In an attempt to steer the conversation to religious things, Nancy said, "I hope you like the evangelist. Have you been to many revival meetings?"

"Some in years gone by, when I was a boy. Dad and Sister used to want me to go with them. I remember that they tried the worst kind of a way to get me to go with them to one just a few weeks before the fire. I'll always be sorry that I didn't go." Blake replied. "You know," he continued thoughtfully, "we owe a great deal to religion and religious folk. I never have been very religious, but I never poked any fun at them. They deserve the respect of the world. There was my folk. They left me a greater heritage than mere money. They left the memory of a life well lived—lived in the strength of a power greater than man."

Nancy was a bit surprised at this from Blake, and pleased as well. He was not all fight and vengeance. She looked at him surveying his well built physique—heavy shoulders, powerful arms, strong calloused hands, a clean cut profile. He was in fact what you would term handsome. She wondered for a minute just how many girl friends he did have. Perhaps one on every lumber job. Yet he didn't seem that type.

"You know, Nancy," Blake continued as he walked leisurely along, taking such strides as to make Nancy almost trot to keep up, "it's too bad we really never seem to appreciate things until it is too late. There is nothing in this world I wouldn't give tonight to hear Dad pray again. Yet, while he was living I used to get impatient about his taking so much time every morning to read the Bible and pray before we went to work. I can remember that more than once he broke down and wept when he was praying that God would help me see my need. I have this consolation, though, I never caused him much worry except what he did over what he called my 'lost condition.' "

"That's all in the past now Charles, and there is the future out ahead. Nothing can change what has already been done. You can live the kind of a life in the future that you think would please your dad and mother." Nancy was taking advantage of an opportune minute.

Blake bowed his head as he walked. There was a moment's silence. "That's about as good a sermon as anyone ever preached to me." There are times when the feelings of the soul won't take shape in words. For Blake this was one of those times. Two feelings played on his consciousness. One was that life had taken on somewhat of a new meaning. He was reluctant to say that it was because of Nancy, but somehow she seemed very much of it right now. The other feeling was somewhat of a sense of awakening of a part of his being he had not felt stir for months, the feeling of obligation to God. There was a sense of incompleteness took hold upon him. He was feeling again the pull of another world. The pull that men will feel when they give the soul a chance to make itself felt. Too often the din of temporal things drown out the voice of the soul until it is heard very faintly if at all.

They entered the little church and made their way down to about the center before finding a vacant seat. It's strange how the ability to walk gives way on folk who come to church. They must tumble into the first vacant seat in the church. The meeting was in progress when

THE WAY OF THE TRANSGRESSOR

Nancy and Blake arrived. The congregation was singing, "Revive us Again." Blake really didn't know the song but he could read the bass notes, taking the higher ones an octave low. Nancy's soft soprano seemed to him about the sweetest voice he had heard since he had heard his mother sing. There seemed to be, in fact a similarity there.

Quick as lightening Blake's mind began to wander. He left the little church, crossed the expanse of years going back to that bleak December night when his mother had called the little group around her bedside to tell them goodby. It was as clear in his mind as though it had only been a few hours hence. His childish mind had recorded every detail of that scene—the saddest a boy ever has to go through—mother's departure. Blake could see his father as he sat at the head of the bed with his arm under mother's head. "Mother wants to see you kiddies," he had said, then with a breaking heart he had listened. "Charles, you be kind to daddy and sister. Daddy will be lonesome when I'm gone so be good to him. Martha, you'll have a lot to look after now. Be strong and brave. I'm sorry to leave so soon. You'll never know how much I love you all, and how much I'd like to see you grown to manhood and womanhood, but God knows best and He seems to be calling." Blake remembered kneeling alongside the bed and kissing his mother's fevered lips and sobbing, "You're the best mother a boy ever had." The smile that played across that pale face was photographed indelibly upon his mind. Martha had kissed her too and they sat down for a few minutes. Blake recalled his father bowing over the

THE WAY OF THE TRANSGRESSOR

bed and putting his rough cheek against the fevered cheek of his wife and whispering to her, "You've been the very best wife a man could ever have. I've loved you more each day. Over yonder, we'll meet in a better world." Sobbing, Blake had run from the room. The next morning dad had said, "Mother left us last night, kiddies. She wanted me to tell you that she would be waiting for you in heaven."

Blake came to with a start. The rest of the congregation was kneeling; he knelt too. But the thought of the calm dignity with which his dad had met every crisis and the faith that triumphed over all seemed to take a new hold upon him there in that little church. As they rose from prayer a number of late comers, Bill Johnson among them, came into the church. Bill sat down alongside of Blake, putting a kindly hand upon the boy's shoulder.

The preacher announced the next song, " 'Showers of Blessing.' Everyone stand please and let us make this the prayer of our hearts that God will give us some real showers here in this place. Troubled hearts need God. Everyone sing."

There was a warmth about it that Blake liked. The man's enthusiasm was sort of contageous. Everyone seemed to take right a-hold of the song. Then the evangelist, Rev. Max Duke began the sermon, taking as his text "There remaineth, therefore a rest for the people of God." He preached a straightforward Second Blessing Holiness sermon. Big Bill Johnson followed every word, drinking in every utterance, comparing it with his knowledge of Scripture. The evangelist was true to the Word; his logic was rather convincing, even to a man who declared that it

THE WAY OF THE TRANSGRESSOR

all came at one time, and that the sin principle remained till death. He closed with several examples of those who had gotten the blessing, and then very pointedly asked, "Have you had the experience?"

Rev. Duke stepped down from the pulpit and stood immediately in front of the folk as he closed his appeal. "A revival is the deepest need of this community. There is only one way to get the favor and blessing of God upon a meeting and that is for everyone to mind God. This may be a little new to some of you folk, but you search the Word and see if God doesn't show you that it is right. Now, I want every man and every woman in this congregation tonight who wants to see a revival to get out of their seats and walk down this aisle and take me by the hand thus saying you'll do your part."

There was a moment's silence; no one moved. Then, Bill Johnson rose deliberately to his feet and walked down the aisle. The preacher felt his hand in a vice-like grip and heard a rough old lumberjack say, "I'll do my part." Nancy followed her dad. Then others came until most of the folk in the church had gone. Blake sat with bowed head while a riot of emotions surged through his breast. He had wanted to go and say that he would do his part but courage seemed to fail him.

When the service was over, they made their way out of the little church, shaking hands with the folk as they left. There seemed to be an interest in each other, and a warmth about the fellowship that made you feel at home.

THE WAY OF THE TRANSGRESSOR

"Do you youngsters want a ride home or will you walk home?" Bill Johnson asked Nancy and Blake.

"I think we had better ride, Bill. It looks like rain and its plenty dark," Blake replied, as he helped Nancy into the car.

CHAPTER IV

THE PARTING OF THE WAYS

October had bid its adiew, vanishing from the list of time. November had come, while the revival still swept on. The work at the Johnson mill had been moving along rapidly; great piles of lumber reflected the autumn sun and filled the valley with a pleasant aroma peculiar to a lumber camp. For some time the big truck that belonged to Bill Johnson was out of order—a broken transmission. It had been a heavy duty job and the parts were hard to find, in fact, they must be ordered from the factory. It seemed that they would never arrive. While the truck was idle, the lumber piled higher and higher.

Other things were developing that were of greater import than the cutting of timber. The battle for the souls of men was raging. Blake had been attending the meetings some; others of Johnson's men were attending spasmodically. Bill Johnson, himself, had seen the need of a pure heart and had gone in for sanctification—and got it. Nancy had followed in her father's steps. Conviction had been deepening on Blake; furiously the battle between right and wrong raged in his breast. The background and heritage that were his made him very susceptible to the Gospel. One thing stood in his way—his hatred for Eric James and his flaming desire for vengeance.

THE WAY OF THE TRANSGRESSOR

Eric James, too, had been to some of the services and he, too, had felt the pull of God upon his soul. God's working upon the soul of any man or woman is a wonderful thing. The sad part about it is that too often the right evaluation is not put on it.

Two men were standing now at the parting of the ways. The decisions were to be momentous. It seems a tragedy that the great decisions of the soul are so seldom seen in their true light. The path to heaven and the path to hell, it seems, are at times not labeled just that way.

It was a beautiful Sunday evening; the November sun low in the sky bathing the hillside with resplendent colors reflecting in a hundred hues of light from the deeply colored leaves of the hickory, the maple, the different oaks, the beech, and then from the green branches of the towering pine and hemlock.

"It's a beautiful world, Blake!" Johnson said as the two walked toward the cabin. "I'm glad too that I know the God back of all this. He is more glorious in the soul of this man than He is in this world of beauty He has created. It is wonderful to have the love of God in your heart, not just in a meager portion, but flowing like a great river. Blake, believe me, you will be wise if you mind God. Is there anything that I can do to help you?"

"No, I think not, Bill. You probably know what the trouble is though. I suppose Nancy has told you something of why I came here and why I've stayed this long. I'm after Eric James. I've vowed that I would have vengeance. I long to slug him until he can't stand on his feet and then choke him until he confesses his part in the tragedy that wrecked my life." Blake spoke slowly and deliberately. "You see, Bill, I am not afraid of James. I would have called him to an open fight long before now if it had not been that I thought I might get more on him by waiting for a while. Now I wish that I had done it before this meeting. Johnson, I now weigh two hundred and thirty pounds. You wouldn't think it to look at me but I do. I want to throw that weight against Eric James and crush him."

"Blake, I know men. You're one of the best built men I've ever seen, and I've seen a lot of them. You could, I don't doubt, kill James with your bare hands in a short time. You are quicker than he; you have much better wind than he. But what good would it do?" Bill Johnson was cornering his man. "I know what it is like to have that feeling burning in your breast. I had it once. Had it not been for the goodness of God in keeping the man out of my reach I would have killed him. Now I am so glad that I didn't touch him. Listen Blake! There can be a lot of real happiness and usefulness in life for you. Don't throw yourself away in this crazy way and maybe land up in the electric chair."

Blake stood with bowed head for a moment. Johnson came close to him as he said, "Blake I think I have a little at stake here. Whether or not you realize it, Nancy thinks a great deal of you. Her happiness means a lot to me. Don't play the fool here. It takes a bigger man to remain silent when wronged than to fight back."

The young giant groaned within himself. Tears came to his eyes. "Bill, I thank providence that I came here.

THE WAY OF THE TRANSGRESSOR

Nancy has brought back pictures of my mother. She would blush to think that I had been bent on the errand I have. Here's my hand on it, Bill. I'm going to change."

Bill Johnson watched Blake walk slowly under the big pine that stood by the shanty, on past the stable, across the bridge and into his cabin. Then turning into his own cabin, he said to Nancy, "Guess I'll not eat tonight. I don't think Charles will be eating either. He needs our prayers now." Johnson walked to the back of the shanty and knelt by his bunk in intercessory prayer.

Nancy slipped into her room and began to pray. She knew of the battle that would rage in Blake's soul. She had the true heart of a woman and knew and felt more than either Bill Johnson or Charles Blake knew.

* * *

We shall not go into the little cabin across the bridge. Blake has gone in there to fight the battle of his life, to settle eternal destinies. He slides the latch on the door, walks to the back of the cabin, falls upon his knees and begins his journey to calvary.

Ham, the old teamster, had found in Blake a real friend. The boy seemed to fill a real place in the old man's life. While it wouldn't be just the way Ham would put it, he loved the boy. As he came slowly toward the cabin he heard Blake say: "Oh God help me to forgive. Take this burning desire for vengeance from my heart." Ham turned and walked slowly toward the stable. He would not break in on Blake. Ham, himself, was feeling somewhat peculiar. There is a sense in which rebellion or surrender is contagious. Blake's surrender to God was having its effect upon another soul—Ham Jacobs. He cleaned the horses, not because they needed it for he had already taken care of that earlier in the day. It would occupy his time and attention for a while. He fed them a little more hay, bedded them, and gave each a lump of sugar before leaving the stable. Then he returned to his cabin. All seemed quiet as he slid back the latch and entered. Blake knelt by the bunk his face turned toward heaven, seemingly oblivious of anything going on around him. Ham hurriedly changed his clothes and left Blake as he had found him. The old log skidder was ill at ease tonight. He went across to the Johnson cabin now. There he could hear Nancy in prayer; Bill Johnson knelt by the side of his bunk. Ham shifted uneasily and then went outside.

"Looks like they're all a prayin' tonight," he said half aloud to himself as he walked toward the boiler where he sat down to watch the fire. "Reckon," he mused to himself, "there must be a God. A man would be a plumb fool to try to deny that. Then, I reckon, if there is a God who rules everything, He must have laws as I've heard them say. It sorter seems reason like that man will live on after this life. It sure enough wouldn't make sense to put them all in the same place when they die. No, Bill Johnson wouldn't belong to the same company that I would I reckon. Guess there must be a little more sense in religion than I ever thought for." He buried his head in his hands and did what too few people do. He did some thinking and reasoning about the things of God. When, a half hour later he rose from in front of the boiler, Ham Jacobs was convinced that the thing to do would be get right with God. Just how to go about it he wasn't sure. But he supposed that about the first sep would be to go to the revival that night.

When Johnson and Nancy came from the cabin Ham announced to them, "Kinder like ter go along tonight, Bill. If there's enough room."

"Plenty of room, Ham. Get right in. It looks like Blake has already gone," Johnson replied.

"He was doing a right smart bit of praying today, I guess," Ham replied.

"I sure hope he's there when we get there", Nancy said as she started the car. "He is having a terrible battle."

* * *

Back in the cabin Charles Blake is still kneeling in prayer. Hours have gone by since he knelt by his bunk—hours of agony, hours of struggle. But now the struggle is o'er; the battle is past; the decision is made. In whispered tones he is saying, "Yes, Lord, I will do Thy will. Not my will but Thine be done." Then in that moment of full surrender a voice seemed to say to him, "Go to the church and I will save you there."

Blake rose from his knees and looked out of the window just in time to see the Johnson car pull out onto the main road. He stood for a moment gazing through his cabin window at the car as the lights faded into the night. All kinds of thoughts flooded his mind. Nancy hadn't been the same of late he thought. It wouldn't dawn upon him that maybe the change was in him. He walked to the corner of the cabin and lit the oil lamp that stood on the shelf. Then he took a note from his pocket. He didn't need to read it, for he knew its contents.

THE WAY OF THE TRANSGRESSOR

"Blake,

You'd better watch that gal. The new Sky Pilot is looking after her. He asked to see her home the other night. You'd better get religion and get her.

Your Beloved,

Eric James"

"I've been a fool all along," he said aloud to the empty shanty. I had no right to think that she ever cared for me. I don't know how it all happened. I never thought of falling in love with that girl. I didn't know that I had until I started to analyze the way I felt about her. Then there is what her dad said tonight. Well, there is only one way out of it." He began to pack his things; he was going to leave. She would soon forget that he ever lived and as to himself, well, he had gotten over other things, he would get over this.

But even as he was placing the things in his suitcase that voice spoke again. "Go to the church." He was not a man to go back down on his word. A few minutes found him on his way to the little church.

The service was almost over when he got there. They were all standing and singing an old song he had often heard his mother sing, "Just as I Am." Without a moment's hesitation, he walked down the aisle, down to the altar. An electric shock seemed to go through the congregation. Ham pushed his way out into the aisle and rushed down to kneel beside Blake. Others followed, until in a few minutes, the altar was lined with raw lumber men pleading for mercy.

THE WAY OF THE TRANSGRESSOR

As far as Blake was concerned things were pretty well settled before he ever got to the church. So he didn't stay long at the altar. Nor did anyone need to lift him up and pump a testimony out of him. He rose to his feet, wiped the perspiration from his brow and said, "I thank God for saving me tonight. From now on, I'm God's man." Others might have said more and made a bigger fuss about it, but they couldn't have been any more in earnest than that boy.

Just then he caught sight of Eric James. He too had been to that final service. Blake meant to settle things right there. James was going out the door. Blake followed him outside. He had planned someday to call James outside, but not just like this.

"Eric! I'd like to see you a minute?" Blake said as he came out the door.

"Sure thing, old boy. I see you are taking my advice. Wise boy!" James' sarcasm was cutting.

"Listen James! I'd like to ask you your forgiveness for anything that I've done against you. I want you to know that you have my forgiveness. That comes from the depths of my heart. I forgive you—everything." Blake felt better already.

That sobered James up a bit. It was more than he expected. "Shake on it. We'll be friends from now on. In a way, I wish that I had done what you did. Maybe some day I will who knows." He turned and walked off into the night.

The battle was over; the last foe was vanquished. Charles Blake was a new man. He felt it, too. He walked

THE WAY OF THE TRANSGRESSOR

leisurely toward the little lumber camp. Coming to a path that cut across a wide curve in the main road, he took a path through the woods that would save him considerable time. Just as he was entering the path two cars pulled past him and vanished around the curve. The head car he knew to be Johnson's but he didn't recognize the second one.

He quickened his pace now for he wanted to tell them that it was all settled. With rapid strides he covered the remainder of the distance. He went straight towards the Johnson cabin. He came almost upon it before he noticed that other car parked alongside of Johnson's. Just then a burst of laughter floated from the cabin. Blake stopped for a moment. In that moment, he saw Rev. Duke pass in front of the window. He saw Nancy go into the kitchen. She was evidently fixing things to eat. Blake had no desire to enter. Perhaps James was right. There was no feeling of hatred. But there was a sinking of his heart as though something had gone from him. He made his way to the cabin across the bridge something like a wounded animal crawls back to its den. He closed the door behind him, and without lighting the lamp, fell on his knees beside his bunk, to fight out another battle of his soul.

When Ham came to his own cabin after the little gathering at Johnson's he found Blake still kneeling by the bunk. He was slowly whispering, "Where He leads, I'll follow."

Blake got to his feet, and greeted his buddy. "Put her there Ham. I'm mighty glad you did what you did tonight."

THE WAY OF THE TRANSGRESSOR

A tear rolled down across the cheek of Ham Jacobs as he stretched out his hand to take hold of Blake's. Mighty glad and happy about it myself, son. Only it seems like I've waited a long time to do it."

"Well, we can't help that now, old boy. Just go at it right now."

"That's what I expect to do, Blake. Here is where I start." Ham reached up on the shelf above the stove and pulled down his weeks supply of "Five Brother's" and threw it into the stove. "Reckon as how I won't be needin' that stuff any longer. Wouldn't feel right chawing on such dirty stuff after the good Lord has cleaned up my heart." Saying this, he tossed the three papers of tobacco into the fire. "I've got a few things to fix up, Blake. Reckon as how I'll need a couple of days off to do it. That pistol hanging on the wall over there, I took from a fellow in a card game one night when he was so drunk that he didn't know whether he was goin' or comin'. And a few other things the Lord has shewed me."

"I'll have a little of the same work to do myself, Ham. I've counted the cost though and I mean to do whatever may be required." Blake spoke with cool determination. "I guess we had better turn in for the night."

CHAPTER V
THE TRAP SPRINGS

Bill Johnson awoke at six o'clock on Monday morning as usual. But when he looked out of his shanty window, he felt a chill run the course of his spine. "Snow!" he said in utter amazement. "There must be two feet of it!" While the night hours had sped by, nature had piled high the frozen vapor from the sky.

Johnson hadn't said much about it, but he was keenly aware of the fact that he was getting into a bad mess financially. That note that James held for five thousand dollars was due soon, he thought, and he had little actual cash to put against it. He had lumber enough cut to just about take care of it, but little cash on hand. Now that the truck was repaired, he planned to rush everything to market just as rapidly as possible.

He climbed out of bed and into his clothes. "I'll not wake Nancy yet, may be we can't do much today." He walked out into the first taste of winter for that year. The snow came almost to his knees as he waded into it. Across the bridge he saw a light in Ham's cabin. He made his way over to where the two most dependable men in his crew were just greeting the new day with their exclamations of surprise.

"Come in Boss. What do you think of this one?" Ham asked.

THE WAY OF THE TRANSGRESSOR

"I don't like it, Ham. But there isn't much we can do about it though. I haven't seen a snow like this in ten years."

"Is there any use in trying to do anything today. I don't think that I could find the logs under this," Ham said.

"No, we'll not try to run the mill today. But I did promise to haul that pile of pine starting today. But I don't know whether or not we can get a road beat to the pile."

"If we had a blade on the tractor, we could soon make a road. I think that we could fix one on all right," Blake said as he finished lacing his high gum shoes. He knew why Johnson was so eager to get the hauling done. The money was needed. "If there's any getting through, we'll get there."

"O kay men. I'll see you at breakfast. No special rush though. The mill won't be running until there is a break in the weather." Big Bill Johnson walked out of the cabin and trudged across toward his own abode. The wind was rising; The snow was whirling in furious clouds that made the whole hollow look like one swirling mass of whiteness. "We'll never make it in this. The roads will blow shut faster than we can open them." He mused as he walked along. "Just as well give it up. Surely God will make a way somehow. Mighty tough to lose everything just over this." But well did he know that should collection start, his little business would crumble. He was not a man easily licked; there would be a way. He had a little time left yet. He sought the refuge of his shanty.

Blake and Ham soon arrived on the scene. "Never saw

the like, for the first storm of the year. You're like as not ter get lost in this blizzard," Ham announced as he came through the door.

"No use to try a thing today, men. It's getting worse. The report is that the wind will rise. That means drifts and more drifts." Bill was plainly pessimistic.

After breakfast the little group joined in worship, each taking a turn at prayer. Ham left to take care of the horses, announcing as he left, "A teamster never gets a day off, no matter what the weather." But everyone knew it didn't make any difference to Ham. The biggest thing in his life had been that team. He prided himself in the roached manes, the polished brass on the harness, the extra gadgets that he had hung all over their mammoth frames.

Bill Johnson went up to the boiler to fix the fire. This left Nancy and Blake alone in the shanty. Blake felt awkward, and embarrassed, for the first time at being left alone with her. He rose to go.

"Blake," Nancy said, "I'm very glad you did what you did last night. I've been praying, we've all been praying that you would do it. Why didn't you stop in here last night? I really wanted to see you."

Blake was thrown completely off balance; he hadn't expected this. Gathering his thoughts, he remarked, trying to appear uninterested in the thing at all, "It looked as though you had enough company last night without me."

Nancy now went on the defensive. How did he find out about the visit on the previous night? Perhaps Ham had told him. "There is always room for you here Blake. You know that." Perhaps she should go on to tell him of the fact that she cared for him—cared more than just a little. But if it was lopsided, and he cared little about her, then why expose her heart to cruelty.

"Thank you, Nancy. It is kind of you to feel that way. But you know that we'll never . . . "

The sentence was never finished. The door was flung open so violently that it seemed to fly from its hinges, as Eric James came buldging into the cabin. "Like to see Johnson. Is he here?"

Bill had seen Eric come to the shanty and had quickly finished his task and started toward the shanty himself. "I'm right here, Eric. Is there something you want?" Bill asked.

"Yes, there is. You could pay me that five thousand you owe me. I need it. You know that note is ten days over due now. If you don't come across, I mean to collect in another way." James was just drunk enough to make him nasty.

"Er—I—I—didn't think that note was due for about a week yet." Bill searched for words while he tried to remember the exact date the note should come due.

"You're a little off there. No use to stall for time. What can you do about that money NOW. You know you borrowed it for just ten months and that is up." James' rage increased as he spoke. He pounded the table with his fist until the dishes jumped around like crickets in a skillet. "There is no use to plead for time," he continued, "I mean business."

THE WAY OF THE TRANSGRESSOR

Bill Johnson was at a complete loss. He had worked mighty hard for everything he had ever gotten. The hospital bills when his wife died had wiped away their few dollars of savings. A fire after that had just about put him to the wall, but he had been able to rebuild his mill and get started again. Now he had enough to satisfy some of his creditors and keep going, if he only had time to dispose of it in a fair way. Just that morning, before anyone else was up he had taken down from a shelf the Bible that had been his wife's. Turning its pages his eyes fell upon this verse, heavily underlined; "All things work together for good to them that love the Lord . . ." Out on the margin were these words, written in the hand writing of one now gone: "I believe that to be true." He had pressed the worn pages to his lips and then knelt to pray. He had been sure that God would make a way, as he rose from his knees. But now the hour had arrived. He didn't have a single straw to grasp for. He merely sunk into a chair and buried his head in his hands, as he said, "I guess you'll have to go ahead and collect, James. I don't have it right now."

"Well, that's just exactly what I'll do. You'd better get ready for it." He threatened as he started for the door.

"Wait a minute James." Blake got to his feet. "I would like to know in the first place where you got that money. But I know you wouldn't tell that. Do you have the note with you?"

"That's none of your business. This is between me and Bill." He moved threateningly toward Blake.

THE WAY OF THE TRANSGRESSOR

"Go ahead Johnson. Tell him to produce the note. Tell him to get ready to write paid across the face of it in his own hand writing. You're going to pay that right here and now!" Blake said as he reached for his pocket. "We can't let a good outfit like this break up over five thousand dollars."

James had been afraid of this. He knew that Charles Blake could easily raise the money. He didn't doubt that he had it on his person then.

The Blake Lumber Company had been a successful company for years. He knew that now Charles owned a half interest in it. Infuriated by Blake's intervention, James rushed at him, intending to drive his fist through his face. Blake dodged the blow, letting the weight of it fall harmlessly on the partition in the shanty. James was now furiously, insanely mad. His eyes were blood-shot; his head leaned forward; a sickening smile played on his white lips. He held his giant fists out in front of him, preparing for another rush.

Blake hadn't wanted a fight. He tried to get out the door, but couldn't without throwing himself open for a severe blow. One full blow from a man like Eric James was more than he wanted to take. He hadn't much time to decide. There seemed to be no choice. He must either defend himself or be beat to the floor by a drunken fool. Now James came at him again. Quick as light Blake jumped from the line of the blow. This threw Eric off his guard. He wasn't used to men fighting like this. Blake watched the blow pass. Then as Eric's arm swung into empty air, Blake sent a mighty upper-cut to Eric's chin. A man

THE WAY OF THE TRANSGRESSOR

weighing two-hundred twenty pounds, all muscle and bone, can swing a tremendous blow. Eric's head flew back, his knees buckled and he crumbled to the floor.

Blake stooped over Eric, raised his head and straightened his neck. He said, "Too bad, James, but you forced me. You left me no alternative.. I'm really sorry that I had to strike you."

James was slowly coming to. Blake put a cold towel on his forehead. But James was cunning. He knew Blake was there by him. He lay still until he was fully to his senses again. Then quick as a flash he whipped a revolver out of his pocket. "I'll teach you to meddle with me." The colt spit fire, once, twice, three times. Blake reeled and fell.

A chair sent hurling through by Ham struck James directly on the back of the head. He went down and out again. The gun flew from his hand. Ham grabbed it; pointed it at Eric and then stopped. "No, God forbids. Two days ago I would have done it. But I can't now." He threw the gun back onto the bunk.

Nancy stooped over the unconscious form of Charles Blake, anxiety was written all over her young face. "Are you all right Blake?" She put her hand over the wound in his shoulder as if to stop the blood. "Can't you tell me you're all right?"

If Blake could have seen the anxiety, the longing in the pair of wide-open eyes that were staring down upon him then, he would never again have questioned the loyalty of the soul for which they were speaking. But he didn't see them, nor did he hear her voice.

THE WAY OF THE TRANSGRESSOR

Bill Johnson and Ham Jacobs picked up the unconscious boy and carried him into Nancy's room. "Get some towels Nancy. Soak them in cold water. I'll get his clothes off and see how hard he was hit," Bill said as they laid him on the bed.

Bill hurriedly unbottoned the heavy woolen shirt and underwear, both already soaked with blood. He raised Blake while Ham slid the clothes down over the wounded man's shoulders. "Looks plenty bad, Ham. But it missed his heart any way. Looks like it may have missed his collar bone, too. Must be only one shot went home at all."

"How badly is he hurt, Dad?" Nancy inquired as she came into the room her hands full of wet towels.

"I'll be goin' for a doc, Bill. I'll get one here as quick as I can," Ham announced as he left the room.

"It missed his heart. He'll pull through all right, if we can get the blood stopped." Keep the towels on his shoulder."

Time and again Nancy took out towels red with blood and brought in others. Big Bill Johnson sat with bowed head alongside of the bed. The bleeding grew less and less. In falling Blake had struck his head on the corner of Johnson's tool box. This explained his lying for so long in an unconscious state. It was several minutes however, before they noticed that there was a gash in his head.

Blake slowly opened his eyes, and stared about the room. "I didn't see that gun, Bill, till it was too late! Did he get me bad?"

"You'll be all right Blake. Just lie still and rest. You

must lie still. Ham has gone for a doctor. He should be back before long," Nancy assured him.

Weak from loss of blood, Blake fell into another doze. Now and then he would mutter something. Nancy stooped close to see if she could catch something he was saying. Once she made out, "I had no right to think she cared." It was enough! The whole thing began to take shape in her mind now. She had given Blake reason to doubt her loyalty to him. It went through her heart like a knife. Falling on her knees beside the bed she pressed her lips against his pale forehead and whispered in a voice full of emotion, "Blake, I do love you. You had reason to think that I cared. I do care. Can you hear me Blake, there is no one else." She buried her head in his pillow and wept.

Thus it was that the moments passed. This division of time into minutes, hours and days is rather mechanical. Minutes are not all alike. There are hours that fly by on wings with the speed of light, when you are surrounded with friends and the air is ringing with laughter, and music is playing in the soul. Then there are moments that drag by slowly, like a wounded snail climbing up grade, when the soul is weighted with anxiety, and the heart is heavy with expectancy. This latter was the kind of moments Nancy Johnson was spending by the bed-side of Charles Blake.

Johnson, who had gone outside for a while, came back in now and found Nancy with her head buried in the pillow. "Is he still resting?" he asked, as he stooped to take the boy's pulse.

"Yes, he hasn't stirred much. How is his pulse?" Nancy asked anxiously.

THE WAY OF THE TRANSGRESSOR

"It seems strong enough; he'll probably make it all right, since he has lasted this long," Johnson answered as he sat down on the bed.

Outside the gale continued to grow in intensity; the air was full of swirling twisting snow. Here the wind swept a patch clear and yonder piled up its gleanings where something broke its force. Giant trees bowed to the unseen power; clouds of loose snow danced like wierd fairies in white across the valley and climbed the hills. It was a day long to be remembered in that section of the country.

Bill Johnson looked at his daughter; her face wore an anxious look. "Nanc, does Blake mean a lot to you?"

"Yes, dad. He means a lot. How much I never realized until today! Do you mind, dad, if I like him—er if I love him!" Nancy looked at her father with questioning eyes. He might well have objections to her falling in love with a shifting lumber jack, even though he was of the better class. But today her mind was catching up with her heart, she knew now that she loved Charles Blake.

Some words suffer because of vulgar usage—like the man on the road to Jericho, they fall among thieves who rob them of their strength and dignity of meaning. Such has happened to the word love. It has been used to describe the shallow, sensual attractions whose duration is about as lengthy as the flash of a shooting star. It has been robbed of its purity and sanctity of meaning and stripped of its worth until it too often suggests the idea of uncleanness, debauchery and baseness. But such was not the love Nancy Johnson carried for Charles Blake. It was love from the pure heart of a pure girl that would sooner die than betray the subject of its devotion.

Slowly Johnson spoke, "Nancy, I feel very full today—my heart is both sad and glad. All of a sudden I realize that you are no longer my little 'Nanc'. You are now a beautiful young lady. I have sheltered you, keeping you from the sin of the age. You have never seen the gay life of the crowded cities, for I have kept you back from its glare. Your mother and I decided that the place to bring you up would be right alongside the old mill, living our plain, simple life. You seem to have been perfectly content with it. You have asked for nothing more. Now I suppose things will soon be different. It is at times like these that I would give all the world if your mother could come back and help guide your young feet through the tangled maze of youthful problems."

Nancy looked at her dad with wonder and admiration. "You're a great one, daddy. I love you—love you because all these years, ever since I can remember, you have lived only for me. I am beginning to know that you have denied yourself much to make it easier for me. How well I remember the valuable lessons you have so patiently taught me. Your wealth of wisdom of the wild has been a constant source of inspiration and amazement to me. Your godly counsel has meant a lot. I have been and still am satisfied with our simple life. I don't think that I'll ever want anything else. But you know, dad, I couldn't help wondering about what the world outside was like. So many of the others in high school keep talking about their plans and about some of the trips they had made and what they had seen that it made me a little anxious to get around a little. But in it all I have discovered that Christ means more to me than the worldly pleasure seems to afford them. There seems to be such a restlessness about that crowd of pleasure seekers; they never seem satisfied."

"I'm glad you feel that way about it, Nancy. You see, I tried the wild life of the world. I was one of the roughest men in this country. Then I met your mother. She was a sweet girl of twenty then, and the prettiest lass I had ever seen. It's funny how I met her. I had just finished trimming her brother. He had been the bully around there until I hit camp. It was destined from the start that we would tangle. It was a fight. She came to me after it was over and said, 'Now, what have you proved? What have you gained? Don't you think there are a lot better things in life than carrying on like a couple of wild beasts?' She was right and we all knew it. Then she said, 'Now, I want to have prayer with you. Get down on your knees while I pray.' I did it, something I had never done to anyone, I got down on my knees. Did she pray! She asked the Lord to put conviction on my heart; she prayed that God would shake me over hell and hold me there until I had enough of it that I wouldn't want to spend eternity there. I'll tell you I didn't feel so high when she got done. I sneaked out of there like a licked dog. Everyone else just seemed to vanish like magic. I got to feeling so bad about the thing that I went to your uncle Tom and apologized. He's been the best friend a man could have ever since. I'd been drinking plenty and was getting worse. There is no telling where I would be now if things hadn't turned. But God brought me down. I got hit with a limb. My arm was broken, my skull fractured, and they thought

THE WAY OF THE TRANSGRESSOR

I wouldn't make it. Well, you know, that girl looked after me. I couldn't help loving her, she was just made that way. She got to reading the Bible to me, got to telling me about hell and the judgment. When I got able to be up, I was beginning to feel how lost I was. I asked her to let me take her to church one night. I had one of the fastest, prettiest little driving horses in the country. She went along all right. That was the night that the old preacher preached me right into hell. It got so real that I thought I would be burned to death right there. When they called for mourners, I was the first one to head for the front, and I did plenty of mourning too. I think they could have heard me for a mile. Oh, but what peace came to my soul when Jesus forgave me of my sins and gave me a new heart. nothing I had ever known could equal it."

Nancy almost forgot herself as she said, "Wonderful daddy! Why didn't you ever tell me that before? But I've found out some more about things, too. Blake told me about some of his experience. Did you know that he had been to college for two years? He was in college when his father died."

"No, I didn't know that. But he did seem much more educated than the average of lumber jacks. Why didn't he finish?"

"Said he couldn't settle down to study after his dad was killed. He decided to hunt down the killer. He felt I guess, that I was sort of hungry for new experiences, so he told me about the college life. What he told me made me feel how little I had missed and how fortunate I was. You have no idea how rotten things are. He told me of the fickleness of affections, of the shallowness of the whole thing. Then he said, 'I think it was my mother's and father's prayers that shielded me from the sin that was everywhere around me. But let me tell you this Nancy, you have more real, unaffected loveliness in your cotton prints than I ever saw in silk and satin on a ball room floor. Stay like you are.'"

Johnson bowed his head. Now, he saw the path Nancy had tread, entirely unknown to him. He could see now the plunging cataracts of despair she had so narrowly missed. His heart was lifted to God in praise that He had safely kept Nancy. "I'm glad you are not wanting to run into that sort of a life, more happy about it than you have any idea. But you know there is a world in which Blake has never lived much as yet. There are Christian young folk, plenty of them in the world. Before you get yourself too much set on any one, you should wait until you are sure."

"You don't need to be anxious, dad," Nancy assured him. "We aren't engaged or anything like that. He has never made any advances toward me in any way. He has always been a perfect gentleman."

"You can tell by the way he acts and talks that he is no ordinary fellow. He has a good background. But he's up to something here, that much I've guessed." Bill said.

"He told me what it was too, dad. He's looking for the fellow that killed his dad. He thinks it was James and figured that he could find out something by staying around where James was. That's the reason he has stayed here," Nancy replied.

The conversation was abruptly interrupted just then, for in came Ham, covered with snow from head to foot.

"No doc today. Not a one will try it in this storm." He announced as he came through the door. "How is he anyhow?"

The booming voice of the old teamster brought Blake out of his doze and he gave Ham the answer to his question, "Better than a dozen dead men yet. Thanks for trying, just the same."

"One doc said as how he would come as quick as he could get through, but knew he couldn't walk 'er." Ham explained.

"I think he'll pull through all right now anyway, if there isn't anything wrong that we can't see." Bill Johnson said.

"Now I reckon as how, I could put away a little grub, Nanc. That is about the worst blizzard I ever remembers seein'. The roads are chuck full most every wheres," Ham said as he began taking off his snow soaked clothes.

"That's right Ham, you haven't had anything to eat for a while. And how about you, Blake? Can you eat a little of something?" Nancy asked as she left the room.

"No, I don't feel like eating anything just now, Nancy. I feel a little weak yet," Blake replied. "Say, will you do me a favor, Nancy?"

"I'd be glad to Blake!" she replied as she came back into the room.

"Drop my uncle a line and tell him about this. You'd better tell him to come down and pick me up as soon as the roads clear. No sense in my staying here and being a burden to you folk."

THE WAY OF THE TRANSGRESSOR

"You're no burden, and you're not leaving for a while at least! But I will write him and tell him if you insist. What is his name and where does he live?" Nancy asked.

"Frank Blake, Hillcrest, West Virginia. Tell him I'm all right though and that I'll need to see him soon as he can come down." Blake said.

"O K we'll do it up just as you say, Blake. Only you aren't leaving this afternoon anyhow." Nancy laughingly replied. It was a laugh she didn't feel. That Blake might leave, had never dawned upon her. She had just accepted him as one who would be staying.

"You see, my real reason for being here no longer exists. I don't want to settle accounts with James any longer. If God wants to do it all right, if not all right. I'm not following the trail of revenge any farther." Blake spoke with feeling.

"I don't want you to think that you are a burden here. Not after what you did for us today especially. Why it is really our fault that you're hurt, so we can surely take care of you." Nancy began.

"No, you owe me nothing. What I did, I did because I wanted to. Your dad is too much of a man to be crushed for $5,000. I have no doubt that it will all come out right."

It was evident that things weren't getting any better for Nancy. She didn't want to expose herself to any cruelty, if Blake were going to go and forget her anyway. Perhaps it was all a one-sided affair. He may have a half dozen different girls. He might be asking her to write to them next.

THE WAY OF THE TRANSGRESSOR

"Uncle Frank has been insisting that I come back right away. He says he needs me to help fill up the hole left by my dad's death. And I reckon it's right, as dad always handled the biggest end of things on the job." Blake explained.

"There is something I wanted to tell you, Blake." Here Nancy began to flush red and she could feel it. She stammered on, "You really didn't have any reason to think I cared . . ."

Just then Ham came booming in the door. "Storm's about over I reckin. Might just go as soon as it came. There could be a whoppin flood out of this yet."

The words died on Nancy's lips. She didn't realize it then, but she would have better not tried to straighten things up.

Johnson came in just then. "Ham, if you'll hitch up the team, I'll take Nancy down to White's for the night. Then we'll not need to move Blake out of that room."

"I'd just as soon take er myself Johnson. It's been a long time since I took a pretty girl for a sled ride," Ham laughed until the cabin seemed to vibrate, and then he slipped easily out into the night.

"Really, dad, I could just as well sleep in the kitchen," Nancy protested.

"Jennie White has been wanting you to come to see her for a long time. This would be a good time to go, when we're not working and don't need a cook. Hurry Ham will be ready in a few minutes."

CHAPTER VI

EASIER THIS WAY

The storm that swept down upon the little settlement, burying it in snow left almost as suddenly as it had come. In a few days the sun and a warm wind had licked up most of the snow banks, turning each little brook into a gushing torrent eager to empty its load into the river.

On Tuesday the doctor had come to see Blake and said that he was getting along just fine. "In fact, there is no reason for me to come back." He had given his permission for Blake to return to his own home the latter part of the week.

The time had gone by all too fast for Nancy. She had determined to tell Blake the whole truth about things but Blake didn't seem to show much interest in her any more at all. He seemed in fact rather cold and indifferent. If she could remember what she had told him, unintentionally, the time Ham had interrupted her, she would better understand Blake's attitude. But that did not dawn upon her until later.

A shoulder wound wouldn't hold a strapping fellow like Blake down very long and in a couple of days he was insisting that Ham help him over to his own shanty. "I don't want to crowd Nancy out of her place," he explained. But the real reason lay deeper than that. If she really didn't care, he would rather not be so near her. It only irritated the wound in his soul.

Ham had taken Blake the food that Nancy fixed for him. She had put forth very special pains to make everything as nice as possible. Sunday noon Nancy had folded a little note in with the napkin she placed on the tray. Blake took it up and read to himself after Ham had gone from the cabin to get his own meal.

"Dear Blake:

I can't understand what has come over you the last few days. We must talk the whole thing over. Could you arrange to come over to our cabin this evening. I must see you.   Nancy"

"Reckon there isn't much to talk over, Nancy," He said to himself. "You have already told me how things are." He ate what he wanted from the generous dinner she had sent him and then put the remainder on the shelf above the table. "I suppose I owe it to her to at least say thanks for the way she has been looking after my physical needs lately." Blake knew that there was to be a youth meeting at the church that afternoon and thus he could not see her until later. Taking his Bible from the table he began to read. He had lots of time during the last week to absorb some of the good things in that Book. He had found that even to a novice its pages yielded sacred treats. He was thus employed a good two hours later when someone knocked at his door.

"Come on in," he shouted.

"Hello, there boy! How are you?" Frank Blake greeted Charles as he came into the cabin.

THE WAY OF THE TRANSGRESSOR

"Hello, there Uncle Frank! I'm mighty glad to see you and no fooling! Just been wondering when you would make it through to get me."

"I started just as soon as I could after I got your letter. Didn't get it until late last night. I saw the post master when I was in town last night and he said that there was a special delivery letter there for me and that I'd better come along with him and get it."

Frank Blake was not a large man, but he was all man. He had stood on the sawyer's platform while a good many millions of feet of lumber had gone over his mill. His hands were drawn from heavy lifting; his back was just a bit from heavy loads. His complexion favored that of an Indian in color. His hair was black as a raven's wing. His eyes, black as his hair and snappy as diamonds, were set wide apart and far back in his head under shaggy eye brows. He was a typical lumberman, a man who had known long days of heavy work, a good many setbacks. He stood there in the cabin, a great example of a man who fought the odds against him without a murmur.

With a sense of satisfaction, he had noted that Charles was reading his Bible but thought it wiser not to say anything about it.

"Are you ready to go?" he asked Charles.

"Just as soon as I throw a few of my things in that suitcase there Uncle, I've been pretty well packed for a couple of days. I don't think that there is anyone at home over at the Johnsons' so I'll just write them a note while you put things in the car. I guess I hadn't better try to carry much of anything except myself."

THE WAY OF THE TRANSGRESSOR

Blake found his pen and a piece of paper while his uncle Frank carried the suitcases to the car. He had seen Johnson and Ham go out the logging road about a half hour before and knew that they were out for a stroll in the Autumn sun. So he would just leave a note.

"Dear Bill, Nancy and Ham:

"Uncle Frank came for me while you were at the church this afternoon and being in a hurry to get back we left immediately. Sorry not to get to tell you goodbye. But it is easier this way. I deeply appreciate what you have done for me here. I wouldn't want James to cause you any more trouble so I am making you out a check for the amount you owe him. You can send me the money when you sell your pine. Do write.

Love to all,
Blake."

"It will be better this way," he told himself as he folded the check up in the note and fastened it to the lamp chimney where Ham would be sure to find it that evening. "I may see her on the way to Wattsville."

In a few minutes things were in readiness and the Blakes were on their way out of the Johnson camp headed for their own mill.

"Been cutting pretty steady, have you Uncle?" Blake asked.

"Every day it's fit for men to be out. But I need you there; the men need a general overseer of the work. In fact, I don't think you should ever have left, Charles." Frank said.

THE WAY OF THE TRANSGRESSOR

"It was a little foolish I'll admit, but I believe it was all for the best though. I got really saved while I was down at Johnsons' though and that is worth it all and more too," Blake replied.

"Your dad was sure a religious man all right. He was always after me about being 'born again' as he said. But I guess that if a man goes to church and gets along with folk he'll make it through all right. I don't really see much sense in this fanatical stuff. But I will admit that they die well when their time comes. There was old Happy Joe as we called him. He got pinned under a tree last week. It was crushing the life out of him. He didn't do any carrying on though. When Jerry got there with the tractor to pull the tree off of him he was just about gone. He said, 'I see the angels coming all right. Ah, yes, there's mom, too.' Then he just quit breathing and was gone. I began to wonder if I could take it like that."

"Well, you know that I was never much for religion, but I really got something in my heart when I went to the mourner's bench the other night. I know something happened in my heart. It was more than just joining the church or turning over a new leaf." Blake testified.

"It may all be that I need a little more myself. Sort o' felt like it since Happy Joe left like he did the other day. He was always after me, too, you know. He said something about we'd all better get ready for the same thing if we wanted to come where he was going," Frank replied. "Say, to change the subject a little, we sure have had some great coon chases this winter. Old Sailor is about the best I've ever seen. We had a great time one night last week. I'll have to tell you about it. The dogs barked treed on a big tall oak on the far side of the tract where we are cutting now, away back over the hill. When we got there we couldn't see the coon anywhere, but we knew he was up there somewhere. It must have been all of fifty feet up to the first limb."

Frank Blake eased up on the conversation while he took a sharp bend in the road, and then began again where he left off. "You remember Jim Close; 'Long Jim' they call him. He wanted to do the climbing. We had along a pair of climbers and he wanted to try them out. He declared that he could climb anything that ever grew. So, up he started. He had no trouble for the climbers were sharp and the bark was smooth. In fact, he got along too good. When he got up about thirty feet he decided that if that coon were up there he was going to stay as far as he was concerned. I was afraid that he would fall off for he was scared. Then he tried to come down. Well, you know how these climbers work. You have to bend one knee and reach down the tree with the other foot, stick that climber in and then pull the other one out. He couldn't get onto that no how. Every time he tried to take a step down he took one up. The more he came down the higher he got. The fellows on the ground were laughing like fools. Pretty soon Jim yelled, 'Where is the reverse on these critters?' Finally we went and hunted up a couple of slim saplin's and shoved them up along the side of the tree and knocked his feet loose and then left him down that way."

Both men laughed with real vigor. Blake laughed too much for he felt the pain return to his shoulder. As they

THE WAY OF THE TRANSGRESSOR

rode along in silence for a few minutes Blake sensed an ache deeper than his shoulder; there was a feeling of ache around his heart as he recalled a lithe girlish form, soft wavy brown hair and eyes that were pools of deep water. He could almost hear her voice now as she said, "You had no reason to think that I cared . . . " That is right. He thought to himself. I really didn't. But there will be work, and more work. I'll get over this, he thought.

The car was eating up the miles, carrying Charles Blake back to the Blake Lumber Company and life in the deep forests. While Uncle Frank was telling the story of the coon hunt, Charles had seen what he thought to be confirmation of his ideas about Nancy and Rev. Duke. Uncle Frank driving fast to get home, had just passed a car that had grown very familiar to Blake, the Johnson car. Blake turned to look as they passed and he noticed that Nancy was not alone. Alongside her was Rev. Duke. Blake gave a little moan; the distance between the two cars widened. Blake didn't look around; he looked straight ahead to the distant horizon. Out yonder, he thought, there will be healing; there will be a chance to forget it all.

* * *

Sunday noon Nancy had prepared Blake's dinner with a great deal of care; she seemed to find a joy in doing things she thought would please him. She had fixed things she knew were his favorites, and had sent generous amounts of them over to the shanty with Ham. Carefully she had written the little note and laid it on the tray in a conspicious place. She had to rush through her own meal to get ready to leave for the afternoon meeting at the church; there was to be a special young people's meeting and she had a part on the program. It was with pleasant anticipation that she looked forward to the evening. This time she would clear from Blake's mind the doubts he held there.

She was surprised to find, upon entering the church, Rev. Duke on the platform. The pastor met her at the door and insisted that she go to the platform too. The chair beside Rev. Duke was vacant and it was the only one left so she sat down.

"How do you do, Miss Johnson," He greeted her. "Glad that you were able to make it here."

"Just fine, thank you. I'm glad to be here." Nancy was at a loss for words.

"Did you get my letter?" he asked.

"Yes, er—I got it." she had too, but it had gone unopened into the kitchen stove. It was on one of those days she was feeling plenty blue over the way things were going with her and Blake.

"Then you'll take me to the train. You were to let me know if you would not be able to do it." Rev. Duke told her.

"No, I really must get back right after the service. One of the men had an accident and I must get right back," Nancy said in a sort of confused manner.

Nancy wasn't good at getting around folk, she hadn't learned that art of easing herself out of a tight place like she was in now. "Why," she thought to herself, "doesn't he see that I don't care for him." Like a flash that phrase brought to her memory the time she had uttered those identical words—told them to Charles Blake. The little moan was never to be understood by Rev. Duke, but he did hear it.

"Did you say something?" he asked, rather embarrassed for noticing her moan of despair.

"No! No!" she said as easily as she could, still trying to get a hold of herself and think just what it was she had told Blake. "Yes," she thought, "That is just the way I said it. I never finished the sentence; Ham came in right then. But I'll tell him what I meant tonight; I'll fix it all up with him." Her heart was beating fast; she felt the blood rush to her face, and then leave again, as she fought to gain her self-control.

"And now," she heard the leader of the service say, "we will be favored by a solo by Nancy Johnson."

Mechanically she arose and walked to the center of the platform, "I would like to sing for you," her voice sounded clear and full of emotion, 'I'm Not Disappointed in Jesus' ". She lost herself in the song; higher and higher rose the tide of the meeting, until when she sat down there were folk all over the church standing and praising God. Some were weeping; some were shouting; some were just waving their hands in the air.

Nancy heard little or none of the sermon that followed. Her mind was on how to get out of that trip to Wattsville. So when the service was over she attempted to get out without being noticed, but there were too many who wanted to shake her hand. They all wanted to tell her how much that song meant to them.

THE WAY OF THE TRANSGRESSOR

"And now we must hurry, Miss Johnson, or we'll miss the train," Rev. Duke was saying. "You folks will excuse us. Miss Johnson is taking me to the train." Nancy found herself being rushed out to the car. She didn't want to protest too strongly here, for everyone knew her and would wonder at such a picture.

She decided that the best thing to do would be to take him and make it as short as possible. Without a word she got the old car into motion—about the most rapid motion it had known in many days.

"Do you plan to go to school this year, Miss Johnson?" Rev. Duke asked her.

"No, I haven't made any plans, at least not yet. I'm not sure just what I'll do yet," Nancy replied.

"You really are a very talented girl, entirely too talented to throw your life away among a bunch of lumberjacks." Rev. Duke went on.

Nancy flushed; he had struck a wrong note there. "There are no finer people on earth than lumbermen, and they need help just as much as any other people. In fact, you'll find that they are a lot more sincere and on the average, a lot cleaner people than the city crowd."

"I meant no offense, to be sure," he went on. "But you really have talent to go over in a big way, to sing to big crowds. I would like you to accompany me on some of my meetings as special singer."

"I haven't the least desire to be great or spectacular. I'll be quite willing to fill whatever place God wants me to fill." Nancy let him know that she wasn't interested in his offers. A car overtook them just then. Nancy didn't see who was in it; she was too busy manipulating the steering wheel to keep the old car in the right lane. The steering wheel had so much lost motion that it kept her plenty busy doing just that. She thought it looked like Blake, but she was sure it couldn't be.

Rev. Duke pressed his case, "I can arrange for you to come to school this winter, if you would only say so. It would really be a shame for you—er to—er—to waste your life—er—cooking meals for a lumberjack."

Nancy was beginning to get indignant. "I'll worry about that!" she said with a tone of finality in her voice.

Conversation lagged now, Rev. Duke decided to bide his time, he had usually gotten what he wanted and just took it for granted that he could do the same as far as Nancy was concerned.

But Nancy felt a surge of relief as she left Rev. Duke standing on the platform and headed the car back toward home. In her mind she was comparing the two men. Duke may be the dressier of the two, but that's about the only point that was in his favor—oh yes he was a minister, but who could tell what Blake might be. At any rate right now she was looking forward to that evening with a keen sense of expectancy.

With light heart Nancy jumped from the old car and ran toward the shanty. She had made up her mind that before long things were going to be definite one way or the other with her and Blake. The misunderstanding would soon be cleared up. She would tell Blake just how she felt about things, and would finish the sentence she had begun once before, but had left unfinished when Ham had interrupted. Blake had a right to think that she cared, for she did, and she saw no need to deny it.

"Hello, Dad. Hello, Ham," she said as she flurried into the shanty.

"Hello, Nancy," Johnson greeted looking up from a little slip of paper he held in his hands.

"Good afternoon, Nancy," Ham added in an absent-minded sort of a way.

"Well, what seems to be so important about that paper, Daddy? You might quit reading it long enough to tell me you're glad I'm home. Not more trouble is it?"

"No, Nancy, it isn't just exactly trouble, but it isn't very good news." Johnson handed the note over to Nancy.

Slowly she read half aloud:
"Dear Bill, Nancy and Ham:

Uncle Frank came for me while you were at the church this afternoon and being in a hurry to get back we left immediately. Sorry not to get to tell you goodbye. But it is easier this way. I deeply appreciate what you have done for me here. I wouldn't want James to cause you any more trouble so I am making you out a check for the amount you owe him. You can send me the money when you sell your pine. Do write.
Love to all,
Blake."

Nancy stood for a moment as if in a daze. She repeated softly the words, "It is easier this way."

"Didn't you get to see him either, Dad?" she asked hoping for a little more from somewhere.

"No, me and Ham were just taking a look around this afternoon for a while and it was just then that Blake left. Reckon his uncle was in a hurry to get going. Sure sorry that I didn't get to see him. But, like he said, reckon it is really a little easier this way."

"Did he really leave a check for that money?"

"That he did. Right here it is," Johnson said as he held up the little slip of paper. "We'll not cash it unless James comes back, and I really don't look for him to show up. He probably thinks that he killed Blake."

Nancy felt sick; the sun left the sky; the clouds of sombre doubt settled down upon her like the Arctic night, and there seemed no possible hope of a sunrise. "I'll change my clothes before I get supper," she said as she left to go to her little room. The tears were very close, and she didn't want them to see her cry.

"You rest awhile Nanc. I'll get the supper tonight. We really don't need much after the dinner you fixed us," Johnson said as he gently slapped her on the back. He knew that there was deep water ahead for her. He watched her go into the room; he wished now, as he had times without number, that Nancy's mother were there to dry her tears and tell her that things would be all right. He seemed so helpless himself in the face of such a situation.

As Nancy walked across the room that was the dining room, living room, and her dad's bedroom toward her own little room in the back, she remembered the car that had passed them as they were going to Wattsville. She remembered that she had thought one of the men looked like Blake as she caught a glimpse of him. She recalled, too, that she had noticed him looking at her as the car went by. The whole thing seemed clear to her now.

Closing the door and falling across the bed, she fled to the refuge of tears. "Why did this have to happen to me?" She stifled her sobs in the pillow. Tired nerves, and an over-worked body, aggravated her torture. She wept herself to sleep.

There is danger in any misunderstanding. It sows the seeds for a harvest of unhappiness, clouds the sky and drives the sun out of the horizon, hushes the song of the bird and drapes the earth with sadness. The more one person means to another, the deeper are the shadows cast by the sombre figure of doubt. Whether there is any reason for the misunderstanding or not does not change the degree of suffering in the least.

Nancy had meant no harm in her associations with Rev. Duke. They had, in reality, been nothing out of the way. Yet she had been willing and eager to explain to Blake, for he had unknowingly and perhaps unintentionally, nevertheless, completely captured her heart. Nancy was willing that it should be so.

CHAPTER SEVEN
ONLY IN THOUGHTS

Nancy no longer looked out the window of the cabin to watch the tractor pull its mammoth loads of logs up onto the skid-way at the mill. Charles Blake no longer drove the tractor. Another man had taken his place. But as the months slowly dragged by Nancy was becoming more and more aware that there was a place in her heart that no other man was likely to fill. It was so empty that at times it actually seemed to ache. November wore away without any word from Blake. She and Ham had searched the cabin that had been Blake's while he was there in hopes of finding an address, but their efforts were futile. Everything was gone.

"Dad," Nancy said one evening as they sat in front of the old wood stove in the center of the cabin and the light coming from the open door cast a halo around the little circle, "can't you remember what that address was that day Blake gave it to me? I wrote it on a letter for him and should be able to remember it, but I can't. I was too excited to remember much then."

"No, Nancy, I can't remember anything only what I told you. And the letter you sent there came back marked 'Unclaimed'."

"It's funny that he would write you a check for Five Thousand Dollars and then never even tell you where to send it back to him. Maybe the check is no good."

"Well, I have never tried to cash it yet. But he wasn't that kind of a fellow. Remember, he had the money in cash the day James shot him."

"Sure Dad. That doesn't make sense." Nancy felt that if the check were no good neither was the man that wrote it and that certainly didn't make sense. Her heart told her that wasn't right.

It was clear to Bill that Nancy hadn't been herself lately. "Don't you worry about him Nanc. If he cared anything about you, he'll be back. If he didn't care, what would be the use in wasting any time thinking about him any way."

"Only, Dad, I am afraid that he didn't understand. You see he felt that I liked Rev. Duke. I really didn't, but Blake doesn't know that. He saw Rev. Duke here that night we had him up for lunch. Then I'm quite sure that he saw me the day I was taking Rev. Duke to the train. That was the day Blake left and I am sure that he and his uncle passed me."

"I see," Bill Johnson said, and he did see. He knew the type of fellow Blake was; he knew he wouldn't play second fiddle to any man, and he knew too that he could very easily put the wrong meaning into what had happened. "Well, things will all come out right. Just pray about it and then leave it to God. You know if you worry you're really not trusting. I can remember how your mother used to tell me, 'Now, Bill, just you remember that you're a child of God, and He loves His children. He won't let anything hurt you more than is good for you.' Many times I have thought about that. It always helped me."

"Yes, I know I'll have to get a hold of myself and do better. But it was a hard blow. He is the first man I ever liked at all, you know. And, Dad this wasn't 'puppy love'."

"You might still find out that it was Nancy. But I'll tell you what, you ought to go to school for a while. Doesn't something happen about January some time, classes change or something?"

"Yes, the second semester begins on the twentieth of January. I just had a letter and some advertising about it the other day."

"Well, then Nancy, that is what you do. Get things ready and you'll be off to school in a few days. Then you'll meet a host of people, and maybe you'll meet one certain one that will look better to you than Charles does. But remember one thing, little girl, you're all I've got in this world, and don't you get so tied up in anyone that you forget about old dad."

"Forget you daddy! That is something. Can we live without air, can the flower live without the sunshine, then I can't forget about you, never!"

The flickering fire painted wierd pictures on the cabin walls. Nancy looked up at her dad. The light of the fire revealed lines in his kind face, there was a little gray mixed through his black hair. His red and black checkered shirt was patched here and there; his heavy wool trousers were chucked down into the tops of the felt boots that he wore. The same low fire burned in his deep set eyes. No she would never forget him, nor that moment.

"OK, daddy," she said at length, "if we can afford it, I'll get ready to go."

THE WAY OF THE TRANSGRESSOR

* * *

"Everything loaded Nancy? Hurry now, or we'll miss that train!" Bill Johnson shouted back into the cabin.

"Coming Daddy." Nancy shouted back. She stepped from her room in a gay little outfit that would make her feel at home among the best. But her heart wasn't so gay. She was leaving her home, even though it had never been any better than a lumber shanty, and she felt it. Carefully she had written a note to Blake to leave with her dad.

"Dear Blake:

If you should come here when I'm not here, I have asked dad to give you this note. Why didn't you write; why didn't you come back? I've wanted to see you! There is so much I want to tell you, but I can't write it. Only remember that I love you—have loved you from the start. Rev. Duke means nothing to me. Blake, I must see you.

Love,
Nancy."

Her father called. Brushing the tears from her eyes she left the room, walked through the shanty to the door. There she looked up the hollow where she and Blake had spent those happy, care-free hours. Oh, for just one more stroll!

"Ready Nancy?" Bill Johnson was in a hurry to get going.

"Ready, Daddy," Nancy said as she ran to the car. They were off. This was to be something new and different.

• * * *

THE WAY OF THE TRANSGRESSOR

The March sun reflected from the melting snow making it sparkle like acres of diamonds. Here and there little patches of bare ground showed through, where the sun hit with hardest force. There was a promise of spring in the air, an invigorating feeling of new life.

A young man clad in red and black checkered shirt and trousers, a bright red cap, high leather shoes swung easily along the path through the standing timber—towering pines that whispered a sad cadence as the wind struggled through their branches, giant oaks pointing like sentinels toward the sky waving slowly to and fro in the March wind.

The soft snow packed under the feet of the traveler as he walked along, head bowed, hands swinging carelessly at his side. He walked leisurely but still the long, even strides carried him swiftly through the timber. Now a cabin comes into sight along the trail, where it bends to follow along the edge of a cliff. The cabin is built on the very edge of the cliff, where some thirty feet below a mountain stream dashes and foams through the rocks, seeming eager to get down the mountain side. The cabin is made from logs, neatly fitted together. The cracks are filled with cement. Over the door hangs a sign made from hickory limbs that artistically delivers the information that the cabin belongs to Blake for the unique name plate reads, "Blakes Lodge."

Blake takes a key from his pocket. "Home again," he said to the empty air as he turned the key in the lock. In a few minutes a warm fire was blazing in the big fireplace. Over the fireplace, on a couple of wooden pegs, hung a Winchester rifle, off to the side, on the antlers of a deer, hung a Colts Automatic. On the other side was the picture of a sweet-faced woman, a young lady, and a man clad in about the same kind of an outfit Blake himself was wearing. A glance would tell you that they were related to the young man who was moving about the cabin. The interior of the cabin was finished in natural oak. The planks were running up and down the wall, beautifully grained and artistically fitted together. They reflected the soft glow of the fire in the fireplace. In the south end of the cabin was a table. On the west wall were cupboards, built over a sink. On the opposite side of the fireplace was a desk and above it were shelves full of books. In the north end of the cabin was a "Bunk", built against the wall. Everything was definitely and distinctively masculine.

Charles Blake had changed a little—his boyishness had mostly disappeared and in its place had come a more manly expression and bearing, brought on, no doubt, more rapidly by the fact that since his return to the Blake Lumber Company, upon him had rested the responsibility of the work. His uncle Frank insisted that Charles do the work his dad had done—general overseer of the work from the stump to the delivered product.

Most of the time Blake spent with his uncle, but over the week-ends and on days when the mill didn't work, he retreated to his cabin, that had been built over his own design. He soon had a steaming meal on the table. Even though it was by now well past noon, Blake hadn't eaten since the early morning. He was hungry and ate like a hungry lion. "Good stuff, if I did cook it myself," he said to the four walls of his cabin. There was something about the afternoon sunlight sifting in through the window that warmed his spirits. He had found a retreat in his work, since leaving the Johnsons. He had tried to forget that he ever cared for Nancy. But still there was a warmth lingered about the very thought of her name.

Blake pushed his chair back from the table and pulled out of his pocket a letter that had been in the morning mail. He pulled a brown piece of paper from the envelope and read the roughly written note:

"Dear Blake:

You may think that the score between us is even but it ain't. I'll be around to straighten it out one of these days real soon. Better be ready. It'll be a fight to the finish this time. You'll wish you'd kept you nose out of my business.

Eric James."

"Fellows like him don't know when they're licked I guess," Blake said to himself. He knew enough about Eric James to know that this was not meant as an idle threat. He knew enough about the man to know there was no limit to which the beast would go to accomplish his end. He recalled the incident in the Johnson cabin months ago. Moving from the table across to the fireplace, he threw another log on the fire, and sat down in a large chair to watch the flames twist and curl. He gave way to something he seldom allowed himself—the thought of days gone by. He seemed to feel the touch of her hand as she stroked the hair back out of his eyes. He seemed to remember faintly her saying, "Are you all right? Tell me you're all right!" Or had he merely dreamed that. A lot of things seemed to be a little hazy about the first couple of days after James shot him. But he remembered distinctly the tender care he had gotten from *her*. But he told himself that she would have done the same for anyone. He couldn't pull all the puzzle together; things seemed so contradictory. If he analyzed one set of happenings he would think that Nancy Johnson did care for him. If he put another set together, he was just as sure that she didn't.

But this he could distinctly remember, she had said it with her own lips and he had heard it clearly, yes, it rang like a bell in his ears, "You had no reason to think that I cared." But as he sat there alone in the glow of the fire he couldn't deny one thing, she was the only girl he had ever loved. "Well, it's all O. K. Nancy. I hope you're having a great time."

Blake dreamed while the shadows lengthened, and as he dreamed his eyes grew heavy. He had been up early and had spent the forenoon out in the cold. The warmth of the fire made him drowsy. Soon slumber had closed out the light of day and closed the real world from view and opened a world of dreams where time and space vanished. Again he walked the trails of the forest with Nancy at his side. Then he was fighting James again and in the struggle he woke himself. He wiped the sweat from his brow. "Whew! Glad to come out of that one!" Then he noticed it was dark. "Night! Already! Let's get to work here!"

Yes, work was a retreat and he had plenty of it to do. Hours later when he put the pen back in the socket, the evening's work caught up, he took his Bible down off the shelf and read several chapters. Then he knelt in prayer: "Oh Lord, I'm so glad tonight for the joy You have brought into my heart. I am so glad for the great peace You have given me, peace that I had never known until you came into my life. Remember tonight the things that are upon my heart. You know about Eric James. You know about Nancy. If it could be Thy will let us meet again . . . . ."

As he rose from his knees he felt the warmth of Divine love flooding his soul; he felt that his life was in the hands of One who was too loving to let things go wrong. There was a delight in feeling that there was a Power interested in your life, a Power that would make all things work out for your good. Just as he was sitting down in his chair by the fireplace the night air was shattered by the blood-curdling cry of a panther. "Old Tom's out again," Blake said to himself. "Wish I could see him over the sights of that gun."

He reached over and turned on the little radio that sat on the shelf by his chair. As it warmed up, an announcer was saying: "And now we are happy to present fifteen minutes of music by the choir of the Northern Bible School. The Choir is under the direction of Harold Bemis. The soloist for the evening is Nancy Johnson."

Blake leaned forward, his mouth seemed to fall open, "You singing in a choir, Nancy!" He listened half in a trance while the choir sang a couple of songs. Then one voice seemed to fill the little cabin—it was the voice of Nancy Johnson. There were a couple more numbers by the whole choir. Then came, "I have a special dedication to make of this last song tonight. I want to dedicate it to my father who is listening and to another very dear friend of mine, who I hope may be listening. This is the favorite song of both, 'Take My Hand Precious Lord.'" Blake leaned forward, placed a hand gently, almost reverently,

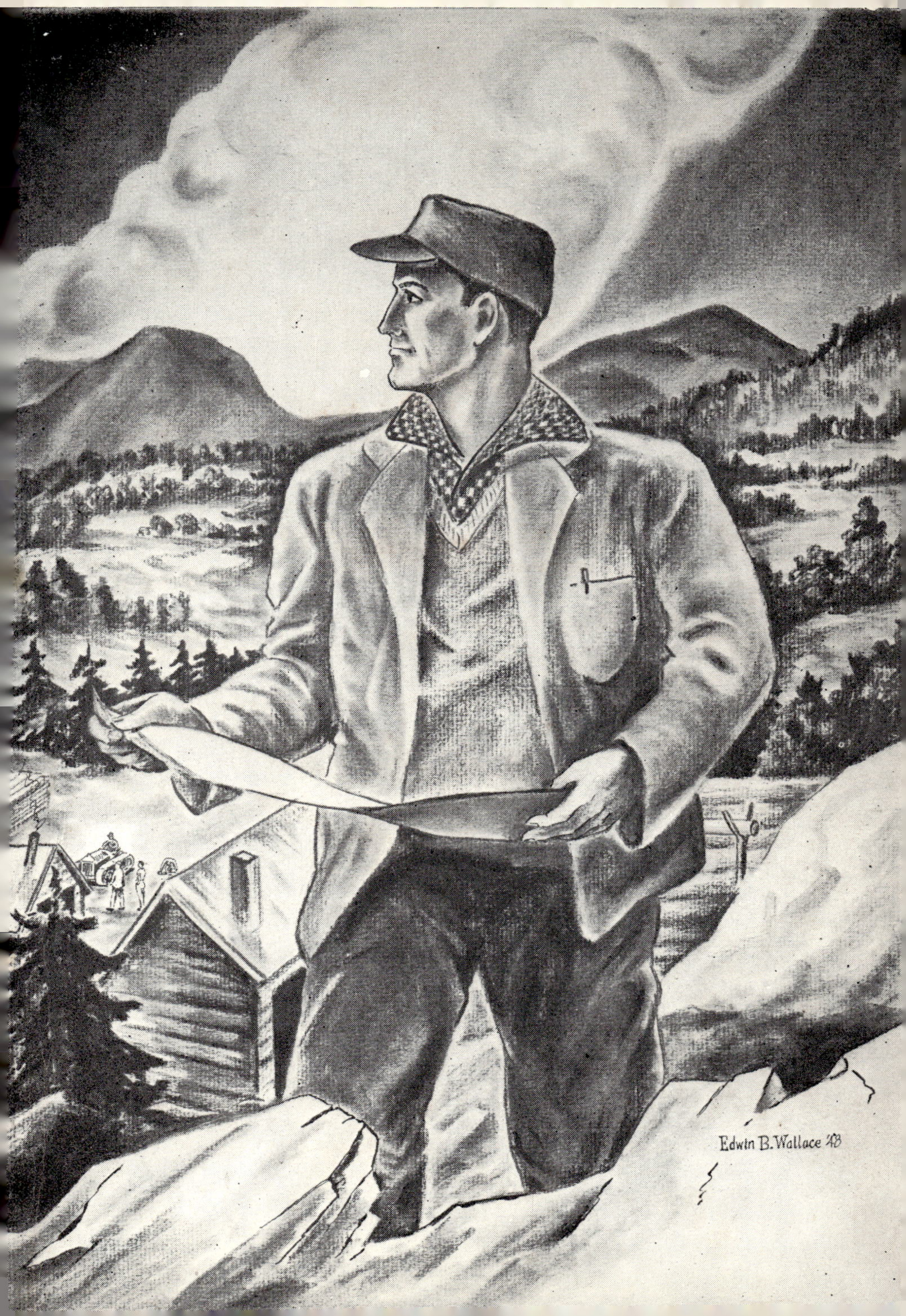
Edwin B. Wallace '48

upon the radio. Nancy was singing the song he had heard her sing during his last week at the Johnson mill. He remembered telling her it was his favorite. As the words floated into the cabin, Blake was seeing a lithe figure in a blue dress walking down a skidding road through the timber, walking by his side. When the last note had died away, he reached over and turned the switch on the radio.

"Nice of you, Nancy," Blake said to the four walls of the shanty.

His first impression was to write her a letter at once, he had remembered the address of the school as given on the broadcast. Then, on second thought, he decided that it wouldn't be the right thing to do. "Nancy is just out of my class and if she doesn't know it now she will later. She just doesn't belong with a lumber jack. Sooner or later she would find that out, if she already hasn't, and what sweeter memories could I have than what I now carry with me. Better leave things just as they are."

Sleep was out of the question. Blake took the Colts from the antlers of the deer and strapped it on. "Here Sailor," he called to a giant Labrador Retriever that lay by the fireplace. Sailor was at his side, and together they walked out into the night. From up the creek "Old Tom" sent out a wierd call into the night air as he scented Blake and the dog. Sailor whined a bit and came a little closer to Blake. Even the dog seemed to sense the ferocity of the beast that was the originator of that call. It was a bloodcurdling scream! An owl hooted from an old tree on the hill top. A full moon sifted light down through the trees to light up the snow almost as brightly as day. Blake walked beneath the towering giants of the forest and seemed to find something that cooled the fever in his soul, stilled the throbbing in his breast. When he had walked for a couple of hundred yards from the cabin, he felt the urge to pray, falling upon his knees he began to talk to God. At first the prayer was general. Then more and more the praying centered around Charles Blake. Lately he had been feeling the need for a deeper experience in his own heart. There had been the stirrings of ill-temper and a feeling of a need for more of God than he knew. At times it had grown into a deep longing. He had heard a few sermons on the topic of sanctification, some one way and some another, until the whole thing was becoming very much confused in his mind. But more and more he was becoming convinced that there was more of God to be had than he was enjoying. There beneath the high sailing moon, in the deep of the forest, with only a dog for a visible companion, and the branches of the trees for a sounding board, Charles Blake began to talk to God about the depth of need in his soul. Deeper and deeper he explored the need. More and more fully he dedicated himself to the full will of God. Finally, when his allegiance to the whole will of God was complete without reservation, he began to see the all sufficiency of the Redeemer's Blood; he began to feel the power of faith lifting his soul heavenward. There came over his being wave after wave of love, the pure love of God. He felt himself bathed in the fountain that had been opened for sin and uncleanness. How long he tarried there he hardly knew; he had become insensible to time. One thing he knew, God had met his soul's need. Theological differences meant nothing to him now, he had felt and the knowledge of experience had overwhelmed every doubt. He wasn't worrying about how to explain it; his heart had felt it. The head could catch up later.

THE WAY OF THE TRANSGRESSOR

With a sudden start, Sailor jumped to his feet. He had learned not to molest his master while he was in prayer. But this time the instinct of protecting his god overpowered all his training and he walked to Blake and continued to growl a low ominous warning of danger. He sniffed the air that came from up the hollow; there was something wrong out there in the night.

"It's all right, Old Boy," Blake said. "It's only Old Tom out there. Let's get back to the shanty." The hair stood up on Sailor's back, and the low growl still lingered in his throat as they started back to the shanty.

What Blake, being a man of the woods, should have noticed but didn't was that the scent troubling Sailor was coming in with the breeze. No animal would stalk its prey in that way. James had promised to visit Blake; destiny had ruled that this should be the night. Out there in the shadows, waiting for Blake, was a man who, having gone over the last barrier from abandonment to evil, was hot with revenge and drunk with both liquor and rage.

CHAPTER EIGHT

THE END OF THE TRAIL

"Sin is a monster of such frightful mein
   That to be hated needs but to be seen,
But seen too of't familiar with its face,
   We first endure, then pity, then embrace."

Eric James was not entirely bad, nor had he always been as wicked as now. Some ten years before, when James was a lad of some fifteen years, his mother, broken in soul and body, died in a lumberman's shanty. Thus out of the boy's life went the only influence for good he ever had. His father was a drunkard, and it was this drinking that caused him to abuse his wife, James' mother, until God, in mercy took her from this life.

The nearest Eric James ever came to anything good was when Charles Blake asked his forgiveness on that last night of the meeting down at the little church near Johnson's mill. There he almost started in the right direction, but paused too long to consider the cost, forgetting to count the cost of rebellion.

He had been a bully all his life. He was a demon for fighting, and until he felt the sledge-hammer blow of Charles Blake's fists in Johnson's cabin that day, he had never gone down on his knees to any man. He did not feel that that score was altogether settled. Hatred boiled in his heart—why he hated Blake, he didn't really know, but the hatred was hot and furious nevertheless.

Immediately following the shooting, he had gotten out of the country for a while. Then he had come back to find that Blake had gone to his uncle's mill. He had sent him a letter telling Blake that he would be calling on him sometime. "The fool ought to know enough to be ready," James laughed to himself. "This time we'll see who comes out on top."

He stopped in at the saloon in town and got just enough liquor to make him reckless and mean. There he had been told by one of the men that worked for Blake that he would find him at his cabin and gave James the directions as to how to locate the cabin. James knew the tract of timber; he had been over it. He knew the trail that led up the stream that came down back of Blake's cabin. It would be an easy task to find it.

The night would be light enough to see his way through the forest and still it would be dark enough to hide him as he carried out his deed. He would meet Blake all alone in the cabin and there they would have it out. Hotter and hotter grew the flame of hatred in his breast as he came closer to the Blake cabin. He ran his hand inside of his jacket and felt the cold steel of the revolver.

The progress of sin in the human soul is a terrible thing; the complete domination of a human soul by the powers of hell is a tragedy beyond compare. The trail that ends in an electric chair often starts in a church during an altar call. When the Spirit of God is grieved out of the heart and life there is no limit to which the powers of hell will drive that soul. Eric James had listened to the

THE WAY OF THE TRANSGRESSOR

devil until his will seemed to be under demon power completely as he slipped through the woods toward his destination.

James paused a moment to rest and light a cigarette. Leaning up against an oak tree he pulled a pack of cigarettes from his pocket. Finding a match in another pocket, he was about to light it when he heard footsteps. Silently he slipped behind the tree and waited. Closer came the figure. Was it? Yes it was Charles Blake! He could tell that easy stride of Blake's any place. James pulled the pistol from its holster and waited—a little more and Blake would cross in front of him! Just as well have it over with! But Blake turned up another trail as he came within a few yards of the tree behind which James was hiding and James was left standing there with cocked pistol and no target.

"Ah, out for a little evening stroll," James chuckled to himself. "Maybe I can beat him to the cabin and welcome him home." That pleased James. He would welcome Blake home. Thus when Blake was out of sight, James hastened toward the cabin, silently following Blake's tracks by the moonlight.

More through accident than anything else, the door was locked, the night latch had clicked into place as Blake pulled the door shut. James found himself locked out upon his arrival. "Nice guy, that Blake" he mused to himself in a drunken sort of a way. "Well, just as well not mess up the inside!" He laughed a grotesque, wierd laugh!

James' mind was so inflamed with liquor that he was now more beast than man. All idea of being himself brought to justice for his crime had vanished, and only the surging waves of hatred wrangled through his soul—flames kindled in by-gone days and re-fueled through the past months now raged with pent-up fury. He would kill Blake; he would stand over him and watch him die. So warped and twisted was the soul of the man that he was going to relish this little bit of work.

"If he would have stayed out of the picture I might have landed my catch. Sure would like to have had her," he thought as he sat down and leaned up against the trunk of a giant pine that stood by the cabin door. It was not a bad place to wait!

Blake would be back, James was sure of that, so he would just wait here by the door until he did come back. He was feeling a little of the liquor he had taken in town. Maybe he had gotten too much. "Well," he said to himself, pressing his fingers against the cold steel of his automatic, "Eric James won't take any chances, Tonight I get my man!"

* * * *

"Big Tom", as the fellows at the Blake job had come to know him, was a huge panther, one of the few that remained of that group of terrible fighting cats that roamed the woods. He had hunted the hills and valleys of the section he claimed as his haunt for five years. During that time he had defended it against all that challenged his dominion.

But now the timber was falling; the deer had fled before the woodman's axe. He was hungry for the warm, quivering flesh of a deer; he was thirsty for warm blood.

The scarcity of game made it necessary that he spend more and more hours on the trail of meat and it meant less and less sleep—sleep that his nervous make-up demanded. He became more and more irritated. Hatred flamed in the great cat—hatred for man, hatred for the sound of the axe and most of all hatred for the roar of the power saw as it purred in response to the cutter's thumb on the throttle.

Many times he had watched this foe of his at work. He had prowled about the cabin that sat on the cliff, watching its occupant come annd go. Ever, always the fire of hatred grew hotter. The hunger for flesh and the thirst for blood became more intense. Blake became the object of hatred and unknown to him Old Tom had stalked him more than once, waiting for a chance to spring upon him and rip the life from him.

He knew this night that Blake had left the cabin but fear of man had kept him from following.

The night air vibrated with the big cat's cry as the scent of man came to his keen nostrils. Like a shadow, without a sound, stealthily he came to the cabin. Often he had climbed the big pine and from its cover watched Blake go about inside those protective walls. Tonight he was desperately hungry; the pangs of hunger and the thirst for blood became so strong that the natural fear of man was crowded to the background.

There in the cover of the big pine, he would hide until Blake came back, then pounce upon his prey! He approached the tree cautiously, stealthily, but rapidly. His agil body glided over the ground as silently as a shadow cast by a cloud. It would only be a matter of time now. He was good at waiting; for hours he had waited for a drink

HE WAS GOOD AT WAITING

THE WAY OF THE TRANSGRESSOR

of blood. He lay close to a big limb that hung out over the cabin, his dark body seemed like a part of the great tree. His green eyes played back and forth like searchlights in the night. His keen little ears were cocked for every sound.

There was the scent of man in the air that floated up the creek. Then came the snapping of a twig. Now the cat could hear the sound of feet crunching in the snow. His agil body grew tense; his eyes flashed flames of green fire as he watched the path. His tail twitched like a live wire. Then came the man! He came directly to the cabin. His hand was on the latch now. The muscles of the big cat tightened like springs under tension. He waited until the man below had settled beneath the tree. Then with a cry that would chill the blood of even a veteran woodsman, his body flew through the air to its victim.

The paths of rebellion against God may not always end on a lonely cliff with a giant panther tearing the life from you, but it will always end in terror and torment. The path may lead through pleasant places and amidst the laughter of friends, but out yonder the lights are going to be pulled from the sky, the night of desolation will surely come. It came for Eric James; it will come for every rebel against God.

The night air was filled with the terrified screams of a man in a mortal combat and the blood chilling cries of a panther killing its prey.

James was hurled against the side of the shanty and dazed by the impact of the powerful cat. It would have crushed most men, but James was a giant and hard as steel.

THE WAY OF THE TRANSGRESSOR

He didn't know what had hit him. But, being all fight, he would go down only when there was no hope. He whipped a knife from his belt and began to stab at the attacker. But he couldn't find a vulnerable spot. He tried his gun but the shot hit him. He put his arms over his face to protect himself a little. Sharp teeth tore at his throat; claws were tearing him to shreds. "Oh, God!" he screamed. Then a giant paw struck him alongside the head and he fell limp to the will of the hungry panther.

* * *

Blake watched the time; he figured how long it would take the old dog to run that half mile, probably less than two minutes. Hurriedly he took down the Winchester, pointing it toward the sky, he fired three shots in rapid succession. Then he waited a moment and then fired three more. That would help arouse his uncle. Sailor would soon deliver the message tied to his collar. The shots echoed through the night. Then he took a giant search light and played it on the sky toward his uncle's home. Those signals Uncle Frank would understand.

Now he took a moment to examine James. The claws of the giant cat had ripped the clothing from his chest and abdomen, and then had ripped the flesh into shreds. Blood flowed from the wounds in great streams. In the center of his chest was a bullet wound. In an effort to shoot the panther, James had, in his drunken stupor and frantic excitement, put a bullet through his own chest. Strange the turn of events! The bullet that was meant for Blake went through the chest of himself. Blake was no doctor, but a glance told him that James would never pull through.

Blood was now upon his lips and foam of blood came out with his gurgling breath.

He opened staring eyes and attempted to raise himself. Blake was wiping the froth from his mouth. "Take it easy, old boy! You'll be all right."

"Oh, God! I'm done; I'm done! That demon got me; God sent that demon to get me! Blake! Blake! Don't let that thing in here! Keep that door closed!" The man screamed as the blood fell from his lips. I'm dying Blake; I'm dying! Do you hear me, man, I'm dying! Can't you help a man when he's dying! Can't you pray; I'm going to hell Blake! Pray!"

There was a moment's silence as Blake again wiped the bloody froth from the wounded man's lips. "There, now, old man, just relax and take it easy. We'll do everything we can for you. We'll soon have a doctor."

"No use, Blake! My time's all up. I'm done Blake. Pray, Oh, pray! I'm going to hell Blake, I feel it now. Can't you help a man when He's about to drop into hell. Look, Blake! Look, there comes the devil now. See him there! I told you not to let that demon in here Blake."

"Now, James, you lie still and I'll pray." Slowly Blake began. It was hard to pray; demons seemed to people the atmosphere. "Dear Lord, Thou didst die upon Calvary for this man. Thou didst suffer that he might be free from sin. Hear . . ."

"Stop Blake! No use to go any farther. I'm most in hell now! I did it Blake; Oh God have mercy, I did it. I killed your father. I stole the five thousand dollars; I set fire to the shanty to cover it up. I did it, Blake! I did it! Now there is no mercy, now there is no use to pray. That was my night Blake, back at the church. That was the last time I felt God at all."

Blake was stunned; words died on his lips. His mind seemed to reel. Here before him lay the man who had blighted his life, had murdered his father and sister. Now the confession had fallen from bloody lips as a soul faced the realities of another world. He breathed a prayer, "Oh, God help me to help him."

"I forgive you, James. God helping me I forgive you! Now then look to God and ask Him to forgive you too." Blake spoke as he tried to get hold of himself. Such a forgiveness would have been impossible but for the grace of God—grace that had enabled him in days gone by to tell James that the deed was forgiven, and to feel it in his heart. The experience of the last hour still burned in his soul, the love of God flooded even now. He could feel its warmth; it was wonderful. James was an object of pity not of hate. Vengeance had taken wings and gone, only pure love remained.

"Can't you ask God to forgive you, James. He is merciful; He will hear." Blake knelt by the dying man as death came closer and closer. Uncle Frank should be here soon, he thought to himself. Yet he knew that human help could never reach James now. He urged James, "You ask God to forgive you."

James was getting weaker. Panic stricken he gazed about the room; he seemed to be looking for an unseen foe. "Blake, I'm done. I'm too far gone to pray. God won't listen to me now."

THE WAY OF THE TRANSGRESSOR

"Yes, He will, James. God will listen if you really repent." Blake urged him to keep trying.

There is no need for an attempt to decide whether the Spirit of God had actually left the man and no longer was there to help him repent or whether fear and pain had so deranged his thoughts that he couldn't pray. The effect was the same—he couldn't touch God. That failure to get through to God would be the sealing of his eternal destiny.

There was a moment of comparative silence, in which the gurgling of the dying man blended with the laughter of the water behind the cabin. It made a weird contrast. Blake went to the door; he thought he heard footsteps. He was right! Uncle Frank and Sue had arrived! How welcome they were! The atmosphere in his little cabin, for the first time, seemed depressing; the moans and cries of the dying man were wearing on him. A soul was slipping into hell and there seemed no help. The gates of doom were standing open and a never dying soul was being pushed through. Gladly would he pull him back from the sulphury pit, but it was beyond his reach.

"Sue, get in there and see if you can help that man any. He's dying in terrible agony. Give him something that will lift the pain a little." Blake pointed toward the door. Sue went in.

"Blake! What on earth happened this man? How did he get so torn around the abdomen; who shot him?" Sue had seen many an injured man, but James was about the worst and bloodiest mess she had seen.

"I haven't had a chance to fix him up any, Sue. He wouldn't let me do anything. He just wanted me to pray for him all the time." Blake apologized for the man's condition. "Is there any hope for him, Sue?" Blake asked as Sue stepped away from James a little way.

"Doesn't look like it, Blake. What on earth happened to him?" Sue replied.

"Never mind that now. Do what you can to make him comfortable, as comfortable as possible." Blake evaded the question.

"Just rest now; we'll soon have you feeling better," Sue assured James as she put the needle into his arm.

"Uncle Frank, do you suppose there is any use in getting a doctor" Blake asked.

Sue stepped back again, after taking the pulse and examining the wound. She answered Blake's question, "No use," she whispered. "He couldn't pull through this." That was the answer.

James seemed to doze a bit; the sedative was beginning to take effect. It was a troubled sleep though. He tore at his breast and shouted, "I'm on fire here, Blake! Can't you talk to God for me? He won't listen to me! Blake hold me! I'm slipping into hell! Here, take hold of my hand; don't let me slip. I'm sorry I did it Blake; I'm sorry I fired that cabin. I'm sorry I killed them, Blake. This is my retribution."

"What! What did he say!" Frank Blake sprang to his feet. "Who'd he kill?" Frank Blake stood over the dying man now. "Whose cabin did you fire!" Vengeance glowed in the eyes of the little man; his fists opened and closed passionately.

"I'll tell you all about it, Uncle Frank. He's getting

THE WAY OF THE TRANSGRESSOR

all that is coming to him. Vengeance belongs to God." Blake's voice was deep with emotion.

Frank Blake strode through the door out into the night, his fists clenched and his head bowed. "He killed the best man that ever swung an axe in this state; he killed my brother!" He walked among the stars beneath the towering trees. The wind seemed to whisper, "Vengeance belongs to God."

Back in the cabin, Sue and Blake stood over the writhing form of Eric James, caught now in the throes of agony both spiritual and physical. Blake watched the facial expressions of the man, now under dope. Misery followed misery in a stampede across the worn countenance. The end came nearer and nearer.

James stared wild-eyed into space. "No, no! You can't get me!" He ducked under the covers and then in a desperate effort tried to rise. "Let me out of here!" But too much blood had soaked the ground outside the cabin and the cot. James was too weak to rise. He clutched and struck at invisible enemies.

"I'm done, Oh, it's hell!" He gasped his last gurgling breath. The cabin was silent, except for the laughter of the little creek, the crackling of the logs on the hearth and the wail of the wind.

Sue spoke first, as she felt for a pulse, "He's gone, Blake. I've seen people die, but none quite like him."

CHAPTER NINE

JOHNSON GETS THE BREAKS

"Big Bill" as Johnson's men had called him had always gotten the rotten breaks. Still his undaunted courage and faith were something inspiring. He seemed to have a philosophy of life that stood the testing and bumps. But now it looked like he had really come to the end of his row.

When he moved on the Kelly tract he had borrowed money to buy the timber, buy a new saw, and a new tractor for log skidding. The sum total of it, after he had paid out what he could on things, was $5,500. He had never been quite so sure of getting things in good shape as he was when he started that job. But one morning in December, after Blake had left in the previous November, the water gauge on the boiler got plugged with some dirt. Jerry, who was firing that morning, didn't notice that the water wasn't bobbing up and down in the glass as it should. He was busy with a lot of things around the mill, getting things started. The steam pressure climbed up and he decided to turn in a little water. The gauge showed a couple inches of water in the boiler, but in reality the crown sheet was dry and red hot. When the cold water from the injector hit that hot crown sheet, the whole country side rocked from the explosion. Jerry, by some quirk of affairs, was hurled out over the sawdust pile, but outside of being badly shaken up, was unhurt.

Tom, the off-bearer, was out unloading lumber, so he wasn't hurt. A piece of the front of the boiler whirled past

Bill, but only brushed him as it went by. The dome off the boiler rode through the air like a kite, coming down almost a half mile from where the mill was sitting.

It would have taken the heart out of most men to see the mess things were in when the steam and smoke cleared away. Bill stood with bowed head looking at the wreck, what was, a few minutes before, one of the finest power plants he had ever owned.

"Funniest thing, Boss," Jerry stammered trying to gain self-control, "There was water in it! I just got through looking!"

"Had you noticed it bobbing in the glass, Jerry?"

"Come to think of it, it did seem rather still. Reckon it could have been plugged?"

"That's about the size of it. But any argument as to why it happened won't fix things up any." Bill studied a moment. He couldn't quit now or things would go to smash for sure and his creditors had faith in him. It would be easier to just quit but he wouldn't do it. "You boys clean things up a little, and watch that no fire breaks out. You can pile up the lumber, too. I'll go into town and see if I can get ahold of a power plant."

So Bill kept plugging. Yes, the old friend at the bank would loan him a little more money. He had discovered that the story James told about Johnson wasn't true.

In a few days the Johnson mill was turning again, turning to the power of a new Diesel engine.

Things moved along smoothly for some time. But Johnson was having trouble moving his lumber. Well he knew that there was a good market for the pine he was cut-

...ıg, but he just couldn't seem to locate any. Then the mines where he had been putting in a lot of lumber cancelled all orders. The coal was running out. Other mines seemed to have suppliers for their needs in the lumber line. Still Johnson kept the wheels turning. He was selling enough to make ends meet, excepting he was getting a little behind on his payments at the bank. But his old friend would take care of that for him, he was sure. The summer came and went. The following winter, just a year after Blake left, was a tough one for Johnson. The driver of the tractor let it get out of control and ran it over a cliff. That was a big repair bill and it meant that the mill didn't work for about three weeks. Some of his best men couldn't wait and they went elsewhere for work.

He kept plugging along through the remainder of the winter. The piles of pine were mammoth, and there were a lot of them.

He had gotten some orders for mine supplies again and was concentrating on them. He was sure that there would soon be a market for his pine. He never had been too good at getting markets. Everyone seemed to want the lumber planed and he didn't have a planer. He was quite concerned about the fact that he was five months behind in his payments at the bank. But his old friend told him to keep paying and to pay up when he sold the pine. He had used up the five thousand dollars Blake had loaned him to pay James, for James had never come back for it.

Spring came, and with it a new determination to make the summer count in cutting the Kelly tract. Then one day in the first of June, just after Nancy had gotten home from Bible School, the blow fell.

THE WAY OF THE TRANSGRESSOR

Bill was out in the lumber yard helping to pile the lumber. A well dressed young man walked up to the mill. "Is Mr. Johnson here?" he queried.

"Yes, sir. I'm Bill Johnson," Bill replied as he walked in toward the mill, where the young fellow was standing.

"I'd like to see you a few minutes, Mr. Johnson. Could we go somewhere where we won't be overheard. What I have to talk about isn't very pleasant."

"Sure, let's go right into the shanty. No one there." Bill answered as he led the way toward the shanty, wondering what was coming now.

"It's like this, Mr. Johnson," the thin-lipped young fellow began, when they were seated at the little table. "my father formerly was president of the bank in Wattsville. You probably have not heard it, but he died a month ago. I am taking over his duties. I discovered that you owe the bank a considerable sum of money and that you have been delinquent on your payments. Your contract states that if for any reason you do not meet your payments, the full amount becomes due and payable immediately. Did you know that?"

"Don't recall ever signing any contract like that, Sir. You must have gotten the wrong man. My contract was just a short one that called for me to make payments each month. Nothing in it about the whole amount coming due if I missed a payment." Johnson moved over to look at the contract the young Mr. Wade was producing. It was an imposing looking document, but Johnson didn't remember ever seeing it before. He had signed a lot of papers in at the bank the day he bought the timber and got the money for the new tractor, but he didn't remember that one.

THE WAY OF THE TRANSGRESSOR

"That is your signature, isn't it Mr. Johnson?" Mr. Wade asked, in mock earnestness.

"Yes, can't deny that. It is my signature." He couldn't mistake his own broad scrawling.

"Well, that means then that I won't be able to sell anything unless I have permission from you."

"That's right, Mr. Johnson. According to the contract, you won't be able to move out anything unless you have our permission. That, you see is to protect us from any chance of your moving out the saleable material and leaving us with no collateral to cover the debt."

"But I have a lot more than is needed for the collateral. All that I would need to sell would be the pine I've got piled out there. It would pay off everything I owe you. You'll give me permission to sell that and pay you off?" The whole thing was a bewildering puzzle to Johnson.

"We would have to approve any sale you made. Of course, if it were for a good price, you could sell, allowing the money to come directly to us. You see Mr. Johnson, in reality liquidation of your place has already begun. You had a sixty day mercy clause in the contract but it has been longer than sixty days since you made your last payment. What you do you must do quick. We'll give you ten days to get the entire amount paid. Am I clear?"

"Yes, thank you. You are very clear. Good day." Johnson said as he led the way to the door.

The world seemed to be falling from beneath his feet as he walked back to the mill — ten days to raise what he owed! Where could he begin?

THE WAY OF THE TRANSGRESSOR

"Jerry, you help the cutters this afternoon, and Tom, you help with the skidding. We'll not run the mill anymore today," Bill told the men. "I've got a little trip to make."

Hastily he changed into clothes that would make him look a little more like the role he was to try to fill. He had always been poor at the selling angle.

"Guess I should have given a little more time to getting that lumber sold and a little less to getting so much cut," he mused as he hurried the old car towards Wattsville.

Some hours later, as the dusk was falling, Bill pulled the old car back up alongside his shanty — a very discouraged man. "Funny thing," he said to himself, "They all seem afraid of that pine. It's really wonderful lumber but they all act like it was full of rattle snakes."

He crawled out of the car and walked up to the mill. Low blue flames shot out of the pile of ashes at the slab dump. Short pieces around the edge of the fire, where there hadn't been so much heat, lay smoldering and smoking filling the whole valley with the sweet aroma of air scented with burning wood. He walked out the lumber tracks and looked at the huge lumber pile outlined against the darkening sky. "A lot of hard work there; too much to loose. This looks like a frame-up to me tonight."

* * *

"Say Chuck, you couldn't guess who just left my office!"

"Wouldn't be surprised it was Bill Johnson, Slim."

"Right! You sure must have given the old boy a scare all right. He offered that pine to me for $40 a thousand.

THE WAY OF THE TRANSGRESSOR

It was a little hard to refuse. Did he swallow the bait, O. K.?"

"Hook line and sinker! He didn't think he'd ever signed any contract like that, but when I showed him the signature, he didn't try to deny it. Clever fellow, that guy we got to copy that signature. But he charged enough for all he did." Chuck Wade and Slim Gaston talked on. They seemed certain of their deal.

"One thing, sure. He'll never get our permission to sell that pine. I've left word at the bank that Mr. Johnson is to be referred directly to me. We'll have to keep this under cover. It wouldn't do for anyone to discover what's going on."

"You'll offer us a lump price for the pine. I'll go for that and we'll split the difference between that and what it's really worth between us. Ought to make a nice little slice at that."

"Yes, I'll be mighty glad to get that pile of pine, too. I've told every dealer around here to watch it, that it was windshaken and rotten. It'll look all right to let it go at a low price." Slim offered.

"The bank will take the mill in and you can buy the timber and whole outfit mighty cheap. He doesn't owe too much and all the Directors are interested in is getting their money out of it."

"If we work this thing right, he'll probably be wanting to stay and run it for me after he has been sold out. It'll be a little hard for him to leave his outfit, so I'll give him a chance to stay," Slim Gaston said. "I've always wanted to own an outfit like Johnson has there."

THE WAY OF THE TRANSGRESSOR

"You be mighty careful you don't talk too much and let this thing out or we will both be in hot water." Chuck warned. "How much pine would you say was there?"

"There's about two hundred thousand feet of it, I would guess." Slim replied. "It's worth $60 a thousand right where it is. It's stuck and part of it is fairly dry. That would be about $12,000 worth of lumber. It's no wonder the old boy got behind a little on his payments."

"He counted on the soft-heartedness of dad. He would never have pushed him. People are going to find out that business is being run in a different way from now on. Let's see. You'll pay $40 and it's really worth $60. That means $20 difference. That means a profit for us of," Chuck did a little figuring on a piece of paper, "$4000 or $2000 a piece. That's worth thinking a little to get."

"It's just as good as in the bag, too, for it's a little hard to sell anything that has a claim on it," Slim commented.

* * *

Bill Johnson kept trying. But there seemed to be no hope. There wasn't a lumber yard in the country that seemed interested in his pine. Finally one lumber dealer said, "I've heard that that pine is not too good. That you've had trouble selling it at all. Looks funny that the dealer right there in Wattsville would pass it up." Bill had walked away. There was no use in arguing about it. He would guarantee every piece of it. They could throw out anything they didn't like. But the more he wanted to sell the less they seemed interested. The time had about run out.

On Saturday afternoon, Bill Johnson called his men into the shanty. He wanted to give them their last pay and

THE WAY OF THE TRANSGRESSOR

then tell them that they would soon be working for someone else. It was going to be a hard thing to break up that crew. Most of them had been with him for years and had stood by through rough and smooth.

The men filed into the cabin. They had heard that everything wasn't as it should be but they didn't think it too serious. Bill had always pulled out before. They found places to sit on the benches in the shanty. Bill stood up and looked at the men.

"This is something that I never thought I would have to say, but it has come to the place where I'll have to let you know that you'll not be working for me any more after today. I'll be leaving this evening or Monday at the latest and the Bank at Wattsville will be taking over the mill and everything. I've done everything I possibly could to keep it from coming to this, but there seemed to be no way out. The lumber that is piled there would more than pay for everything I owe, but I can't get it moved in time."

"How much do you need, Boss?" Ham Jacobs asked in his usual blunt manner.

"I'll need ten thousand dollars, Ham. Need it before Monday at ten o'clock."

Ham blinked a little as he replied, "Reckon as how I wouldn't be able ter do nothing as big as that. Sure be glad to let you have what I got. Got one thousand over in the shanty."

"That's mighty great of you, Ham, but it wouldn't help much. They are demanding the whole thing. Sort of slipped one over on me, but can't do a thing about it now." Johnson spoke with emotion.

THE WAY OF THE TRANSGRESSOR

Others volunteered, but the whole that they could scrape together was less than two thousand dollars. Johnson knew there would be no use to offer that to the young banker. If it had only been his dad, things would be different.

"We'll start up again, Johnson. This two thousand we can scrape together and a little credit we could get would get us started in a small job. We'll all stick with you; work for just enough to keep us alive until things get moving again." Jerry spoke up.

"Sure thing, Bill. I know where there's a little tract of timber that can be bought for a couple hundred dollars down. I know the fellow real well, he'll let us move in on it for a couple hundred and pay the rest as we go along," old Bob, the log cutter spoke up.

"We'll see about that men, but let's think it over until Monday. It will be mighty hard starting from nothing when you're as old as I am. The lumber business is really a young man's game."

Every man took Bill's hand as they left and declared that they would stay together. Old Bob said he was going to see the fellow that owned that timber and get an option on it that very night. Ham declared that he would go along and lay out any cash that was needed to seal the bargain.

"No, don't put out any money on any timber until you've had a chance to go over it. That wouldn't be good business." Johnson felt a little foolish talking about good business now.

As they were leaving the shanty a car pulled up alongside where Johnson's was parked and a man Johnson did not recognize came toward him.

CHAPTER X

BIG TOM STRIKES AGAIN!

Charles Blake was a busy man! The Blake Lumber Co. was growing so rapidly that it kept him jumping to keep ahead of things. More and more things were resting upon his shoulders. The orders must be looked after, the cutting overseen, the delivery kept on schedule. Then he put in a kiln to dry the lumber and a planing mill. They were putting out high class material there on the Blake job. But the many duties kept him from his thoughts, which was just as pleasing to him. Spiritually, he had grown by leaps and bounds. He was now supporting two native workers in India and planned to add a couple more. In his heart burned a passion to tell others of his Christ. He had hoped that maybe he would be called to preach, but that never seemed to materialize. He seemed to get one answer, "God needs lumbermen, too."

Through the spring and summer he had seen things take great strides on the lumber job. He had added a couple more trucks, bought a three hundred acre tract of timber that lay next to the tract they were cutting. He had put in a new Diesel engine to run the mill, bought a new and bigger 'cat'. He had the best crew of men to be found anywhere around in that section, for he paid them well and used them right.

Things were mighty fine, excepting that he couldn't forget. He couldn't forget that there had been a brown-eyed girl named Nancy Johnson. No, he hadn't heard a word from her for over a year. He hadn't tried to contact her, and as far as he knew, she hadn't tried to contact him. That later was perfectly according to his expectations; she had told him he had no right to think that she cared.

With the coming of the next spring after James was killed in his cabin, Blake decided that maybe he should look up Johnson and see how things were going with his old friend. "After all," he said to himself, "he does owe me that five thousand dollars. In fact he really owes me ten thousand. And with all the expense, I could use a little of it anytime now."

But weeks passed into months and still Blake had never gone to see Johnson. The days were full of things that demanded his time. The evenings were partly taken up with speaking engagements. He took every occasion to help others to Christ. His messages were straight from the shoulder and they rang with a sincerity that made them persuasive. He was much in demand as a young people's speaker. When there were no speaking engagements, there were numerous other things to be taken care of. During the summer he and his Uncle Frank were going to open up a lumber yard in an adjoining town, this was taking considerable planning.

Finally on a June afternoon as he walked back through the woods to his cabin on the cliff, he decided that it was time to hunt Bill Johnson. Something seemed to tell him that he should go to see his old friend. It was a very pleasant walk back through the timber. The birds were singing, the trees were in full foliage, giving cool shade to the passer. There had always been melody in the sound of the forest to Blake; this afternoon it seemed to be a very symphony of beauty. A Blue Jay scolded as he

THE WAY OF THE TRANSGRESSOR

passed too close to the nest; a squirrel sitting on the limb of a giant red oak, barked a warning and retreated into a hole in the limb, overhead a crow gave out its warning caw that an invader was passing through their domain. Yes, there was melody in them all for the lumberjack.

But still, he wasn't exactly content. There was that vague, indefinable feeling, that longing for close companionship. "Funny thing," he mused to himself as he walked along, "but it looks like the whole world hinges on love. I never saw it so plainly before." He stopped a minute to watch a couple of robins build their summer home. They had probably already raised one nest full of young, now they were preparing to raise another.

There was nothing wrong about it. Only it didn't seem that any of it belonged to him, or ever would. Not that there weren't plenty of girls that would be mighty glad for the chance, but he had seen one that topped them all, and couldn't stop comparing the others with her, which, he decided, wouldn't work out too well. But that didn't take away the desire for companionship, something he had very little of. He lived alone, thought out his own problems, carried his burdens without any earthly help. It seemed at times that he was foolish for going on like that. But when he thought of Nancy, others didn't measure up. It seemed that at times he could see her in the evening shadows. The fire in his fireplace on wintry evenings reminded him of the light that ever seemed to slumber in her eyes.

The renegade would commit his darkest crimes for the companionship, even though he couldn't have the love, of a woman. The pioneer endured the privations of the rugged life, the dangers of copper colored savages, the uncertainties of the untamed country that he might have the joy of living for and loving his mate. The Indian brave, when not on the war path, walked hand in hand with a soft-eyed maiden over the forest trails and told her of far off voyages, craggy mountain summits and sunsets on distant and beautiful lakes.

"Build it well, there Red Breast," Blake said, putting his field glasses to his eyes to get a better look at the building process. But as he began to focus them something else caught his eye over on the other ridge. He could see four people lounging in the shade of "Stable Rock." It had been named that because, some of the early settlers had stabled horses under it when they first came into the country. An old trail one time had gone out over the ridge.

"Some campers, I reckon." Blake said to himself. Then he paused. What was that sneaking up to the top of the rock? There could be no mistake as he watched it sneak along close to the ground like a shadow, silently, stealthily, "Old Tom!" Blake gasped.

He raised the Winchester, but lowered again without shooting. It was too long a shot. The bullet might strike the rock and glance. There was but one thing to do, dash across the creek ascend the ridge and come up from below. If only time didn't run out! If only Tom waited. Blake covered the ground like a borderman, swiftly, silently. There wasn't a twig snapped. Rains had softened the forest floor. He had reached the creek, coming out where he had planned at a narrow channel. A giant leap and he cleared the stream. Powerful muscles, steeled by work carried him up the ridge. He stopped to look. Tom was still there. A little closer now.

THE WAY OF THE TRANSGRESSOR

"Wait!" he almost said it aloud. The cat was crouching for the spring. His tail twiched, a few seconds and it would be too late. "Better try!" Guickly the rifle swung to his shoulder came up steadily, paused and then spit fire. The giant cat leaped through the air! "Missed!"

Every ounce of strength was called out now, speed was urgent. Blake ran as only a man like him could. With giant strides, he covered the ground. His chest heaved and fell as he breathed, but there was no slackening of the pace. A little more. He drew his knife as he ran. It may be a hand to hand encounter.

Below the rock there was general screaming. Blake saw two fellows and one girl running, stumbling down the hill. "Must have got one!" he thought. He grabbed a root and swung himself up to the ledge below the rock.

Directly in front of him the big cat lay motionless in a heap. Just along side it lay a girl-unconscious. Blood flowed from her left arm and above the elbow, and the right leg just above the knee. Blake bent over her.

"No! Not you Nancy! It can't be you!" Excitedly Blake felt for a pulse. It was O. K. "Thank God," he breathed. Gently he brushed the hair back from her forehead. A cut above the left eye explained her unconsciousness. She had struck a rock when she fell.

Blake cupped his hands to his mouth, "Come on back, you cowards. Give me a hand." Blake had put two and two together in a moment.

Gently Blake picked up Nancy, a tremor ran through his giant body as He pulled her up in his arms. Fate was

E. B. Wallace 48

playing a dirty trick on him, he thought! As rapidly as he could he carried her to the cabin—his cabin. She was no load for a man who every day taxed his muscles hour after hour in manual labor. He laid her down on his bunk. Then turning to the others who had come back and were following, Blake said, "Go on in and stay with her until I get help."

Blake was again bounding through the woods. It was Saturday afternoon. "Sue should be home." he thought as he ran. "Uncle Frank can go for a doctor."

* * *

"You go on in Sue, I'll wait out here. If you need me call," Blake opened the door to his cabin and pushed Sue in through the door way.

Nancy still was unconscious an ugly bump showed on her head. Sue took her pulse. It seemed all right. Then she examined the cut on the arm and leg. They were nasty slashed but nothing serious. It was evident, however that the bump on the head had been quite severe.

"Hope we don't have a fracture, here." Sue said to Jean. "What's your name?"

"Jean Matthew. We were at the lodge over the ridge," the girl replied. "We were just resting by a big rock up on the ridge, when that horrid creature came hurtling down on us. Sure lucky for us that that lumberjack happened along when he did."

"Yes, that was rather fortunate." Sue said. "Those fellows you were with wouldn't have shown much fight if that panther had dropped in on you without a bullet in him, judging from the way they ran from him when he was dead."

Jean didn't answer, she was plainly ashamed of the boys.

Cold applications and ammonia were bringing Nancy out of it. She opened her big eyes and stared about the cabin. "Well, where am I? Where's the rest of the gang; did that panther kill anyone?" she questioned.

"No, honey, you are the only one that he touched. You see he was dead when he hit you." Sue relieved her fears.

"Dead? What killed him?" Nancy asked still staring in wide-eyed bewilderment.

"A bullet killed him. But you just be still. We'll talk about that later." Sue quieted her. "Does your head hurt, honey?"

"It sure does. It feels like it's split right through the middle." Nancy said.

"Well, we'll hope it's not that bad, Nancy," Sue encouraged.

"Say now, tell me, who you are and where I am will you?" Nancy begged.

"Well that really doesn't matter. Just call me Sue, and you are in a lumberjack's shack right over the ridge from the lodge," Sue told her.

THE WAY OF THE TRANSGRESSOR

Blake had made Sue promise not to disclose her identity or the identity of the cabin. Sue agreed that it would be best to keep her from knowing for the time being.

"It's funny, Sue, but I thought I saw an old friend of mine running toward me just as that panther struck me. It looked like Charles Blake," Nancy said. "But it couldn't have been."

"It's queer how things like that get into our minds at times like this, but you just rest now and things will be all right," Sue replied, trying to cover any surprise she felt. "The doctor should be here before long, so you try to get a little rest now." Sue pulled a blanket over Nancy and then went outside to where Blake was waiting.

"How is she, Sue?" Blake asked immediately.

"She's mighty nice, at least, Blake. And she's very much alive. And, too, she thinks she saw you running toward her just before the panther struck her." Sue was enjoying Blake's reaction.

"Reckon, she could have caught a glimpse of me as I climbed off the boulder I was standing on when I shot. But don't let her know!" Blake pleaded.

"Might be the best kind of medicine for her. The doctor may perscribe it. Blake those are sure a pair of beautiful eyes she's got." Sue laughed.

"Here comes Doc." Blake said pointing down the path.

"Hello, Doc. Nurse here before the boss again," Sue joked. "Right in here."

"Say this is where you had your experience with James, wasn't it?" the doctor questioned.

THE WAY OF THE TRANSGRESSOR

"Yep, this is the place. Sort of getting his cabin in the spot light isn't he?" Sue replied.

"What seems to be the trouble?" the doctor asked as he walked over to the bunk.

"The worst thing is her head, Doc, I've fixed up her arm and leg. They're just minor cuts."

Nancy was dozing again as the doctor walked over to the bunk. "Best keep her awake. Here young lady, what's happened to you?" He laid his hand on her head and Nancy opened her eyes. Skilled fingers pressed here and there, felt the ridges and bumps. May be a light fracture; may be just a bad bump." No danger unless concussion develops. Considering the difficulty involved in getting her out of here, we'll just keep her still for a while. Can you stay with her Miss Blake?"

"Stay as long as necessary, I guess, Doc. Don't start on my next case for a few days yet," Sue informed him.

"Fine, keep that big boy Charlie handy so he can run for help, if you need it. Here are some pills for the pain. I'll be ready to come if needed." Doc said in a matter of fact way as he left the cabin.

"Well, what's the verdict Doc," Blake asked.

"Nothing serious, I think, my boy. Where's that cat?"

"Up on the ridge, where I shot it, I guess. Want to see it? I'm going up and tote him down. Biggest that ever came to these parts — I'll bet on that."

"I'll stick around for a few minutes, while you bring him in."

"O. K. Doc. I'll be right back" Blake said as he bounded off across the hollow.

THE WAY OF THE TRANSGRESSOR

In a few minutes he returned with old Tom. He had taken the front paws of the cat and put them one on each shoulder. The head lay back over; the hind feet of the panther touched the ground. Blake was six feet two.

"Man, what a beast!" Doc exclaimed, moving up to Blake. "Let Sue see that critter! Sue look out here once."

"Charlie! Is that the panther that struck Nancy? It looks more like a lion than a panther."

"Some do call them mountain lions, but this is an uncommonly big one," Blake said as he laid it down under the big pine. Right here is where it got James. Reckon he was really waiting for me that night. Think I'll have him mounted."

"Well, I must get going. Call if anything develops," Doc said as he started down the path.

"Listen, Blake, Nancy is asking all sort of questions. She heard Doc call me 'Miss Blake' and you 'Charlie' and she's putting two and two together. You'd just as well come on in and have it over with," Sue said as she led the way back to the cabin.

"Reckon, I know a little about the way John Smith felt. I'd rather face old Tom than try to straighten this out. But here goes!"

"Brought you a visitor Nancy. Here's the owner of this domain, Mr. Charles Blake."

"Hello, Nancy. Sure glad to have you drop in. Sorry it had to be on such a mix up though." Blake was trying hard to appear natural.

Nancy just said one word, "Blake!" she was near to tears at the best. Now they came.

THE WAY OF THE TRANSGRESSOR

Blake felt as out of place as a bull in a china shop. "Turn about's fair play, Nancy. I took your cabin over one time. And what a nurse you made, too. Best any man ever had."

"Thank you, Blake. Forgive me for being such a baby. I'm just upset that's all."

"I had Uncle Frank go for your dad. He's on his way here now. Told him not to be worried though."

Sue spoke up, "Blake I worked all night last night; you keep Nancy company a while. I want to take a little snooze."

"You go right ahead, Sue. I don't need any attention. I'll call if I need help."

Blake didn't know how to take that. It went home in the wrong way.

"I'd like to hang up that Panther. Really ought to skin him. But I'll let the fellow who mounts him do that," Blake said as he left the cabin.

He hung the Panther from a limb on the old pine. Then he sat down and watched the evening fade into twilight and then into night.

Suddenly it dawned upon him that there were no lights on in the cabin. Sue must be sleeping. He opened the door quietly. Nancy was sobbing. Quickly she gained control of herself again.

I'll turn on this little table lamp. It won't be so bright in your eyes," Blake said.

"Is your head hurting too bad," Blake asked as he walked to her bed. "Wish I could be as good a nurse to you as you were to me, Nancy."

THE WAY OF THE TRANSGRESSOR

"That's all right, Blake. I owe my life to you now. And dad and I owe so much to you to begin with. And on top of all that, I'm afraid I made you unhappy." That was as far as she could go. Tears came in floods.

Blake was at a complete loss. He didn't know where to begin. He pulled a chair up to the bedside. "Nancy, you must be quiet. We'll talk this all over, later."

"I'm all right, Blake. My head isn't hurt that bad. It was fright more than anything else. It was terrible seeing that monster flying through the air at me. I was froze. I couldn't scream or move. I had no business out here."

"I'm glad you did come here, Nancy. It gave me another chance to see you."

"You knew where you could see me, Blake, if you had wanted to."

Her words were very clear to Blake. He bowed his head just a bit. Then replied, "I didn't think you would be wanting to see me. It appeared to me that your interest was elsewhere."

"You might have given me a chance to explain. There really was an explanation to it all. Do you want to hear it now?"

"No, I guess not Nancy. It doesn't make any difference." Blake was afraid to carry any conversation very far with Nancy feeling as she did now.

"It does to me, Blake."

"I mean—er—if you say that there was a reason I'll take your word for it. You don't need to explain, not just now."

THE WAY OF THE TRANSGRESSOR ....

Blake was feeling more and more embarrassed and was getting into a corner fast. Nancy had come out there in the company of another young man who that very minute was probably sticking around somewhere, and would no doubt soon be calling to see Nancy. The torture of soul he had gone through was something he didn't want to revive. He woke Sue and told her he had a little business in town yet that evening. He got his slouch hat and was about to leave when Nancy called after him.

"Blake, will you do me this favor—go to the lodge on the lake and tell the group that I won't be going back with them. Tell Max Duke that I would rather he didn't come here to see me. Tell him that I'll write him when I'm feeling able to do it."

Blake turned crimson, but kept his voice in perfect control, in spite of his surging emotions. "I'll certainly do that for you."

"I think that was the gentleman who came here a while ago, when Blake was after the panther, and I told him he wouldn't be able to see you for at least a couple of hours," Sue said.

"When I come back Sue, I'll just sleep on this cot here. You can sleep in the room next to where Nancy is. I'll not be gone too long."

CHAPTER XI
THE WAY IT GOES

"Mr. Johnson, I guess." Frank Blake put out his hand.

"You are right sir," Bill replied as he held out his big calloused hand.

"I'm Frank Blake, Charley Blake's uncle."

"I'm glad to see you; that I am. Won't you come into the shanty and sit down."

"No, I came down here on a little errand. Charles sent me down here to get you. It seems that Nancy was hurt this afternoon. The school youngsters were having their outing. Nothing serious, I understand, but Charles thought you ought to be there," Frank explained. He knew it was sort of blunt, but he wasn't much of a diplomat. About all he knew was to say it and let it be at that.

"Just what happened? Did you hear how she got hurt?" Johnson asked anxiously.

"Seems like a panther that has been prowling that section jumped off a rock and struck her," Frank told him.

"I'll be ready in a minute," Johnson said as he retreated into the cabin. He was going to get ready to leave anyhow. He almost welcomed this opportunity to get away from things over the next day. He had been dreading it. Nancy wouldn't be home; he would be sold out on Monday, so the prospects were not too bright. "Nancy hurt!" he repeated to himself as he got a few things together. "Sure hope it's not bad." In a few minutes he had rejoined Blake and they were on their way. The two found

THE WAY OF THE TRANSGRESSOR

plenty for conversation, as they had so many things in common, except that Blake was a man secure in his business, and Johnson was at the end of the trail. The fact that he owed Charles Blake five thousand dollars rested like an iron weight upon his chest. He didn't see now how he could ever face him. There just didn't seem to be any way to remedy the situation. Blake didn't have so much as a note. It would be no use to make one out now.

As the car sped over the miles, the conversation within it turned to religion. The two men were discussing their views of theology in general.

"Well, I never thought much of religion, for a good many years," Frank Blake was saying. "I never did anything against it, but just figured I didn't need any of it for myself. I wanted to see the church go all right, but never did much to help it go. Then my brother died in that fire, or he was killed and then his cabin fired, to cover it up. That made me think. I knew he was ready to die, for he had been a religious man for years. He had gone 'forward' as he called it in a revival meeting. But when that sort of wore off, I still didn't do anything about it. Then, a while back, we had a man get crushed under a tree. He was one of the fellows that had got religion the same time my brother did. You know, Johnson, that man didn't seem to be afraid to die at all. He was just as calm as anything. Then I got to thinking again. Supposing that had been me; how would I have acted? I would probably have been hollering like mad for someone to pray for me. Then, right after that, Charles came home with a real dose of religion—never saw it make such a change in anyone—and he started working on me. Well, it just all piled up until I decided that the thing to do was get a little myself. So, I went to the mourner's bench in a little church out our way and got the real thing. Now Charlie tells me that there is another Blessing 'er something that I am needing. What do you think about that?"

"About the best answer to that," Bill replied, "Is that I got it and that I think everyone ought to have it too."

"Well, I always said there was no argument as good as that. If I'm on the outside of something good, I reckon as how I'll be wanting to get on the inside track and get it."

"There is a lot of theology I don't understand, and never will," Bill went on, "but I guess experience is better than theory any day."

"That's right. And one good testimony is worth a lot of so called proof, as far as I'm concerned," Frank replied.

Frank Blake pulled the car off the road, "The trail to Blake's cabin is right up along the creek there. This is about the closest we can get to it. I'll take you up and then take the car on around home."

"So we're here already. I'm going to be glad to see that girl again," Bill said as he got out of the car.

The moon was full and bright; the two men had no difficulty in finding the path up to the cabin. They talked as they walked, and thus didn't notice that Charles had pulled his car in just a little behind them and was following them up the trail. He walked faster than they did, so that he overtook them before they reached the cabin.

"Hello there, Boss. It is mighty fine to get a hold of that paw again. I haven't felt one just like that since I left down there," Charles welcomed him.

"And it feels mighty good to get a hold of yours again, Blake. You're bigger than ever, aren't you boy."

THE WAY OF THE TRANSGRESSOR

"Gained a little, not much. Only weigh two hundred and twenty now."

"It's just like having a good-sized horse around, to have that fellow on a job. He's just a copy of his dad. A little bigger I think." Frank broke in.

"This is no time to be talking about our waist lines. Let's see how everyone is in the cabin," Blake said as he opened the door.

Sue and Nancy were talking.

"You girls still chewing the fat," Blake said as he turned on the lights in the outer room. Here Nancy, we brought you a man you'll be glad to see."

"Why, daddy. I didn't expect you tonight. I didn't think you would try to drive up here in our old car after night. But how glad I am to see you. Never been so glad in my life."

"Don't think that I've ever been so glad to see anyone myself, as I am to see you and Charlie here." Johnson said as he took Nancy in his arms. It had been so long since he had had any fellowship with one he loved, that seeing Nancy and Charles was like getting a new lease on life. For a while at least he was being lifted clear above his troubles.

"You don't look too badly disfigured Nanc. Where did the brute hit you?"

"Here on the head is the worst place. I think I hit my head on a rock when I got knocked over. That was the worst scare I ever got or ever want to get."

"It all proves that we constantly need Divine care, Nancy. Are you all through with school?" Bill asked.

THE WAY OF THE TRANSGRESSOR

"All except the graduation; but I won't be going back to them, so, I guess you could say that I'm all through. I'll be mighty glad to get back home again, Daddy. Just back there in the old shanty to cook for you will be all I want for a while."

"You're not planning to do something else right away?" Johnson didn't know, with things stacking up like they were whether that was good or bad.

"Not for a while, at least. Had an offer to teach in a little Bible School for next fall. I may take that, but it isn't definite. How are things going at the mill?"

Johnson searched for words. "We've had a little more trouble than usual lately, little trouble to get the right kind of a market for that pine. But it could be worse."

"Things will all come out all right; the Lord has always proved Himself in the past. He won't fail now." Nancy seemed confident.

Johnson felt a little ashamed of himself. He had tried hard to save the situation himself, but while he had prayed some, he had not really laid out his need before God. "It's too late now," he thought to himself, but he wouldn't tell her until the last minute.

Blake came into the room, putting an end to the conversation for the moment. "I'm going to go with Uncle Frank for the night. Johnson you just take over and make yourself at home. I have a service in the morning and one in the afternoon. I'll be dropping around toward evening tomorrow. Uncle Frank will be around in the morning, to see if you need anything. I'll leave my car parked down at the road, just in case you need it. Here are the keys. I'll let Sailor stay here. In case you need me in the night,

THE WAY OF THE TRANSGRESSOR

Sue knows how to send him for me." He paused a minute; he thought he could read disappointment in Nancy's eyes. She couldn't be wanting him to stay for a while! That chap to whom he had delivered her message had brushed him aside, and informed him that he was going to call to see Nancy Johnson in the morning. The whole thing took on puzzling aspects. He was moving out of the picture. Looking toward Nancy he said, "Now you get a good night's rest. Good-Night!" With his easy moving stride he was about to go out the door.

"Wait a minute, Blake. Remember I told you that there was an explanation to what you saw, to what you heard, to everything. I must tell you."

Blake's heart pounded like a trip hammer. He suddenly became uncomfortably hot. He kept his voice in perfect control, "Well, Nancy I always give everyone a chance to say anything to me they want to. Then I reserve the right to draw my own conclusions. Some things are pretty evident here. You go to sleep and we'll talk it all over sometime soon." With a smile Blake was gone from the room.

It suddenly felt empty and hollow. There was a change came over the whole place when Nancy knew that Blake had gone for the night. "I've been such a fool, Daddy!" She sobbed. "But if he won't listen to me, and I can't blame him if he doesn't, I want you to tell him for me that I've always loved him and always will. You know that Daddy."

Johnson bowed his head. He had been married to a girl like Nancy, for that girl had been Nancy's mother. He knew that nobler heart never beat in the bosom of a woman. Her's had been the love that brightened every day of his life while she lived and cast a hallowing aroma about his life even in her death.

"Yes, Nancy, I'll talk to him. Things will all work out all right. You know what you told me about the mill!"

"That's the way it is; you always seem to be able to tell others how they should trust and then can't seem to do it yourself." Nancy wiped her eyes and then said, "I'll quit being such a baby. I'll make him listen to what I have to say, at least."

"It's terribly late, Nancy. I'm going to curl up out on Blake's couch. You go to sleep now. I'll be right out here if you need me."

* * * *

"Good evening folks. How are provisions holding out?" Blake came bounding in the door. Seeing Nancy sitting in his big chair, he said, "Well, it seems to take more than a bump on the head to keep you down for long. But then you're the daughter of a lumberjack, so that's about what I'd expect from you. Mighty glad to see you sitting up, little girl." He seemed in high spirits. "Had two of the best services today, I ever had. The Lord did give us a couple of great cracks at the devil." His eyes lingered a bit on the slender girl in the big chair. He'd get rid of that chair when she was gone. He wiped his brow as if to wipe away a mental picture. No, it could never be. But it would be wonderful just the same to see her there in that chair in the evenings,—waiting for him, to come *home*. He wheeled on his heel and went into his room to change clothes.

"It's been a long time since I cooked for you two," Johnson said as Blake came back from his room. "But I've made myself at home here and scraped together a little meal. We've sort of hoped you'd get home in time to eat with us."

"Say, it really looks good, too! Where did you get that steak? I didn't have any of that around here. In fact I completely forgot to lay in any provisions on Saturday night. Excited I guess."

"Your Uncle brought that over this afternoon. Mighty nice of him too." Nancy said.

They sat down to eat. The sunset over the western hills was something no language could describe.

"The sunsets aren't always that beautiful here, are they?" Nancy asked.

"Oh no, not every night. But they are most of the time. It's the formation of the hills, I guess." Blake said. "This is a great place to live here. Tomorrow, if it works out so I can, I want to show you our plant here. How are things going for you, Johnson?"

"Not so good." Johnson bowed his head. He may as well tell them. Blake had a right to know. "Guess I'll not be in the lumber business for long. At least not for myself. It's mighty hard to say it, but-er, well I'm being sold out tomorrow morning at ten o'clock. She'll soon belong to somebody else."

"Dad! I didn't know it was that bad. You mean there is to be a sheriff's sale? Our mill is to be sold!" She began to feel dizzy.

"They framed me down at the bank, closed in on me before I had much of a chance."

"Wait a minute here. Don't you have a lot of pine down there?" Blake asked.

THE WAY OF THE TRANSGRESSOR

"A nice lot of it, Blake. You know that there never was any nicer pine than that we're cutting down there. There hasn't been a stick moved either. I couldn't sell it in time." Johnson spoke with resignation. There would be no need to go into the whole story.

"How much do you need, and when do they take over?" Blake shoved his chair back from the table and faced Johnson.

"I need $10,000 before ten o'clock tomorrow morning. I can't get it anywhere. But I'm worth twice that much. The pine alone is worth more than that. There's a lot of timber on that tract; then there's all that equipment. But what is the use in thinking of that now! It's too late. Do you think you could use me here, Blake?"

"We're not doing any business on Sunday Johnson, but you're not done yet. We'll get that money around to them before the dead line. This thing looks like a crooked deal to me. It looks funny. Most places they would go along and give you a chance to pay it off. But you forget it for this evening. I'll think out some way to fix this up. I'll buy that pine and give you the cash for it."

Johnson looked into space for a minute. Nancy sobbed. She wiped her eyes and said, "I told you there would be a way, Daddy. But I didn't know it was going to be such a big amount and that things were near so bad. But there was a way."

"You are mighty fine, Blake. I'll never let you down." Johnson took a hold of the boy's hand in a clasp he would never forget. He thought he had a grip, but that Bill Johnson's! I already owe you for the time you saved me before. I'll have a chance to pay that back now too. Say, you know James never came for that money!"

THE WAY OF THE TRANSGRESSOR

"No, Johnson and he never will. James is dead. He died right here in this cabin. The worst death a man could die, torn to shreds by the same panther that almost got Nancy. He had come here to kill me. But he confessed that he stole that money from my father, that he had killed my father and sister. So you don't owe him anything."

"He's dead! 'The Way of the Transgressor Is Hard'. But I owe that money to someone. It would rightly be yours then." Johnson seemed a little dazed by the swiftness of the developments.

"We'll not worry about that right now. Let's finish supper. While we've been talking all this good stuff here has gotten cold. But here we go just the same." Blake began to pass things around. They had forgotten about supper. "It's sure a treat to see you folk again. You don't know how glad I am to see both of you. It's been a long time since I've had as much enjoyment as this, having you two here for supper. It will be a bright spot to remember for months to come."

"Now since we found you boy, you're going to see us more often. Why under the sun didn't you ever come down to see us? You knew where we were located. Nancy has liked to pine herself to death." Johnson looked at Blake.

Blake looked at Nancy. Her face was a bit flushed, but Blake could see no wavering in those eyes. Things were really getting bewildering. "I suppose I should have gone back, but thought it would be best not to do it for a while. Then . . ."

"Blake, why did you think it wouldn't be best to come for a while?" Nancy asked.

THE WAY OF THE TRANSGRESSOR

Blake avoided the question. "Say, who shall we call in to do the dishes?"

"Never mind the dishes. I've been doing my own for two years now so I reckon as how I can take care of these. You young folk might want to talk a while. You go right ahead. I'll clean up the things here."

"I would like to take a little walk, to get some fresh air. Sue said I could when you came back this evening. She said you should take me for a little walk." Nancy had wronged him, innocently but nonetheless actually and she was determined to set things right. He probably would never care for her again, but she would tell the whole truth just the same.

"I never rebel against orders, although I hardly recognize Sue as my superior. But here we go." He helped Nancy to her feet.

A mellow moon was just about half way up over the hill when they stepped out from the cabin door. A fox barked down the hollow; from across the ravine came the answer. Nancy and Blake stepped out into the luxuriant evening air, ladened with the fragrance of the forest.

"This is a beautiful evening." Nancy opened the conversation. "It's grand to be out again, after two years in the stuffy city."

"I imagine it would be great. Never spent much time in the city. The college I attended was in a sort of country like place. This section of the country is really beautiful. The only thing about the lumber business that I don't like is that we turn a lot of places like this into old briar slashings."

THE WAY OF THE TRANSGRESSOR

"I've often heard Dad say the same thing. But still the country needs lumber, and this is the only way to get it."

They walked in silence for a little while. Then Nancy continued, "Blake, we'll probably always live in two different worlds, but there are a couple of things I want to straighten out just the same."

He had thought the same thing, but he hadn't expected her to come out with it so plainly. "Yes, Nancy, I know that. Which explains why I never came back to see you—I mean that is one of the things. I'm nothing more than a lumberjack. That's about all I ever will be. You are a talented girl. You have a real future. I had hoped that I might get a call to preach, but the Lord seems to be directing me in other paths. I'm reaching folk that way that would not be reached by any other way. Then I have been able to give considerable to the Cause. The Lord has blessed this work in a financial way."

"Blake, you don't see what I mean." She slipped her hand in his. A tremor went through him. They walked in silence a moment. "I mean that Dad and I are poor. We always will be. We will probably never get out of debt. You have money; you are successful. That, Blake, is what I mean by living in different worlds. But what I want to explain is something else. What was among the other things that kept you from coming down to our place?"

Blake began to stammer for words. "Well, I guess, I thought it would just be better if I didn't."

"Now, Blake, we are going to get this thing all straightened out tonight." Nancy pulled her hand from his. He didn't resist. She had a feeling that she shouldn't have been so forward. "I'll probably never mean a thing to you. But

THE WAY OF THE TRANSGRESSOR

I want to be understood. You remember when we were talking just before you left. I told you that you had no reason to think that I cared . . . I never got the sentence finished. Ham came in then. You never gave me a chance to finish. I was to blame, too. I was a coward. But tonight I want to finish that sentence."

Blake stopped and looked at Nancy. Above, the limbs of the pines sifted down the light from the moon. That sentence seemed finished enough. It seemed final. Blake remembered it just as well as though it had been that afternoon.

"Here is the rest of it . . . for Max Duke. That, Blake, is the end of that sentence. It was true then. It is true now. There is something else." Nancy continued. She could talk now. Words came easy. She had perfect control of herself. Blake seemed frozen into a statue. "You saw me with Max Duke that Sunday afternoon. I was merely taking him to the station because I couldn't get out of it. You had no right to think wrongly about that. I was with him here on this trip. This is the last. I don't love him; I never will. There is one more thing I want to say, Blake. I've loved you through the last two years, even though I have never seen you. I love you still tonight. That is all. Let's walk back to the shanty."

The world seemed to reel for Blake. He tried to find words but they didn't seem to come. He took Nancy's hand. His thoughts were clearing. "Nancy, you completely take me by surprise. I had thought all along that . . . . Never mind what I thought. It was all wrong. But still Nancy you are a talented girl. You can fill a big place in life. You shouldn't tie yourself down to a lumberjack like me."

THE WAY OF THE TRANSGRESSOR

"Blake, you had a sister. What would you think would have been her ambition in life, if she had lived?"

"She wanted to do the Lord's will, whatever that might have been. She always said that."

"That doesn't always mean to preach or sing. It means to fill your place for God's glory where ever that might be. Blake, don't you know that the noblest place a woman can fill is being a Christian companion to a noble man and a godly example in her home?"

"You mean Nancy that you would—that you would—that you would marry a lumberjack?"

"Not just any one, Blake. It would have to be a very special one."

"Would I do?"

"You're the only one that would, that I ever saw." Nancy felt herself being swept off her feet in Blake's arms. Never was purer love given nor purer love received.

* * * *

"Say, I was about to send out a tracing party after you two," Johnson greeted them when they came back to the shanty. "But when I think of what you've done for us, Blake, I guess I'll not strap you tonight." Johnson laughed like he hadn't laughed for months. He wasn't going to lose things after all. "You'll never know how much I appreciate this, Blake. I just got to thinking things over. This will save me from a terrible blow. But I'll pay it back!"

"That's all right. If you'll give your consent, it'll all be in the family anyhow," Blake shot at him.

"What's that?"

THE WAY OF THE TRANSGRESSOR

"Daddy, he's asking you if he can marry me?"

"That's too much for one day. What's that verse in the Bible? 'The way of the transgressor is hard, but the way of the righteous grows brighter and brighter'. That may not be exactly like it is, but that is just exactly like it works."